Presented to:

_____

By:

_____

On:

_____

Presented to:

_____

By:

_____

On:

_____

GNT
Children's
BIBLE

CATHOLIC
EDITION

Good News Translation

Zonderkidz

GOOD NEWS TRANSLATION, SECOND EDITION,
Formerly known as Good News Bible in Today's English Version
Copyright © 1992 by American Bible Society.
Used by permission. All rights reserved.

Deuterocanonicals/Apocrypha: © American Bible Society 1979, 1992.
Revised introductions to Daniel and Baruch © American Bible Society 2001.
Maps: © United Bible Societies 1976, 1978.

GNT Children's Bible, Catholic Edition
Copyright © 2002 by The Zondervan Corporation.
All rights reserved.
Imprimatur
†Most Reverend William H. Keeler, D.D.
President, National Conference of Catholic Bishops
March 10, 1993

Library of Congress Catalog Card Number 2002100039

Grand Rapids, Michigan 49530, U.S.A.
Printed in the United States of America.
All rights reserved.
http://www.zondervan.com

02 03 04 05 06 07 08 09 10 /DP/ 10 9 8 7 6 5 4 3 2 1

Contents

Alphabetical Listing
with Abbreviations

Foreword

The Good News Translation of the Bible seeks to state clearly and accurately the meaning of the original texts in words and forms that are widely accepted by people who use English as a means of communication. This translation does not follow the traditional vocabulary and style found in the historic English Bible versions. Rather it attempts for our time to set forth the biblical content and message in the standard, everyday, natural form of English.

The aim of this Bible is to give today's reader maximum understanding of the content of the original texts. The Preface sets forth the basic principles which the translators followed in their work and explains the nature of special aids for readers.

The Good News Translation was translated and published by the United Bible Societies for use throughout the world. The Bible Societies trust that the reading and study of this translation will result in a better understanding of the meaning of the Bible. We also earnestly pray that readers will discover the message of saving faith and hope for all people, which the Bible announces anew to each generation.

What it Means to Be a Catholic

Dear Kids,

Here is a Bible just for you.

As a Catholic, you, your family and the members of your parish community listen to the readings from the Bible at Mass. This collection of readings is called the lectionary. The readings are from the Old Testament and the New Testament and change each week during a three-year cycle. You also study and read from the Bible in your religion education class, or faith formation class.

Now here is a chance for you to read the Bible on your own, with your friends and with your family. This Bible is for you. It is written in a way that you can read and understand.

The Bible is a story of God's love for all people. In the Bible we learn about God's great love for us and how we can love God and others.

One part of the Bible that young people really enjoy are the stories of Jesus. These are found in the Gospels of Matthew, Mark, Luke and John. When you read the Gospels, you can learn all about Jesus' life, His work and His message. Jesus teaches us how to live, to love God and to love all people.

As a Catholic you also learn about your faith from your parents, adults and when you go to religion classes. You learn about the Mass, prayers for everyday, the seven sacraments, the Ten Commandments, the Beatitudes, the lives of Jesus, Mary and the saints. You also learn that as Catholics we believe:

In One God, the Father, the Almighty, Maker of Heaven and Earth
In One Lord, Jesus Christ, the Only Son of God
In The Holy Spirit, the Lord, the Giver of Life.

One of the best summaries of what we believe as Catholics is found in the prayer called the Nicene Creed, which Catholics pray at Mass. Turn to page xviii if you'd like to read it. You may also have heard the Apostles Creed before, which is also a good summary of our beliefs. Turn to page xvii if you'd like to read it.

As Catholics we all belong to the Catholic Church, the community of God's people. As members of the Church, God invites us into relationship with him through prayer, the sacraments and the Mass. God calls us to be disciples and followers of Jesus Christ.

We hope and pray that as you read this Bible, worship with your family and parish at Mass, and learn about your Catholic faith at home and in class, you will know that God loves you in a very special way and that Christ Jesus is the way, the truth and the life.

Daniel J. Pierson

Dan has worked as a Catholic school teacher for five years, parish director of religious education for nine years, and as a diocesan director of religious education for seventeen years. He received a Masters Degree in Religious Education from Loyola University Chicago.

How to Use This Bible

Welcome! Are you ready to start using your Bible? Check out all these great features:

The Good News Translation
The Bible text itself is the most important part of this Bible, because it is God's Word, written for you. The GNT is a modern translation, and it is very easy to understand. It's written at a 5th grade reading level. This Bible includes the Deuterocanonical books such as Tobit, Maccabees and Wisdom.

What it Means to be a Catholic
Turn back a page and you will find a letter that is written to you. It will help you understand what it means to be a Catholic and how being a Christian can be the biggest and greatest adventure in your life.

Book Introductions
At the beginning of each book of the Bible, you'll find helpful information, including an overview of what happens in the book and what that means to us as Christians. The introduction will also give you an outline of favorite Bible stories and teachings you can find in that book.

In-text Pictures
Nearly 600 line drawings by illustrator Annie Vallatton help you see and understand all the different scenes and events in the Bible.

Full-Color Illustrations
Beautiful artwork by Robert Sauber will show you some very important events in the Bible. See page xv for where to find them.

Catholic Prayers and Blessings
On the back of the full-color artwork, you will find favorite Catholic prayers and blessings. Do you know some of them already? Turn to page xvi for where to find them.

Four-Year Lectionary
If you would like to read the passages of Scripture that will be read aloud in church for the daily and Sunday Masses, just go to the back of your Bible to the lectionary on page 403. This schedule makes it easy to find the correct readings simply by looking at the calendar date. The liturgical years (beginning with the first Sunday of Advent—usually occurring late in November) are also clearly marked so that you can follow the church calendar as well.

Maps
On page 347 in the back of your Bible, you'll find all sorts of maps. Check out what Jerusalem looked like in New Testament times. Or trace Paul's journeys to many countries. The map index on page 361 will show you where you can find each map.

Subject Index
Want to look up "Abraham" or "Angels"? Or how about "Jerusalem"? Look in the back of your Bible on page 365. The subject index will tell you what these words mean and will tell you where you can read about them in your Bible

Word List

What does "Apostle" mean? Or how about "Sickle"? Check out the answer in the back of your Bible on page 335. This word list tells you what objects and cultural terms mean so that you can better understand what life was like in Bible times and what it means to you today.

Other Features to Check Out

Chronology of the Bible

Prayers of the Bible

Miracles of the Old Testament

Miracles of Jesus

Ministry of Jesus

(Turn to the Table of Contents at the beginning of your Bible to find where these are located)

It is our prayer that you'll get to know God better as you read this Bible. We also pray that the Holy Spirit will work in your life so that your relationship will God will grow stronger and stronger.

If you have any questions or comments about this Bible, please write and tell us:

Bible Editor

Zonderkidz

5300 Patterson SE

Grand Rapids, MI 49530

Index to the Illustrations by Robert Sauber

Index to the Illustrations
by Robert Sauber

Index to Prayers and Blessings

Index to Prayers and Blessings

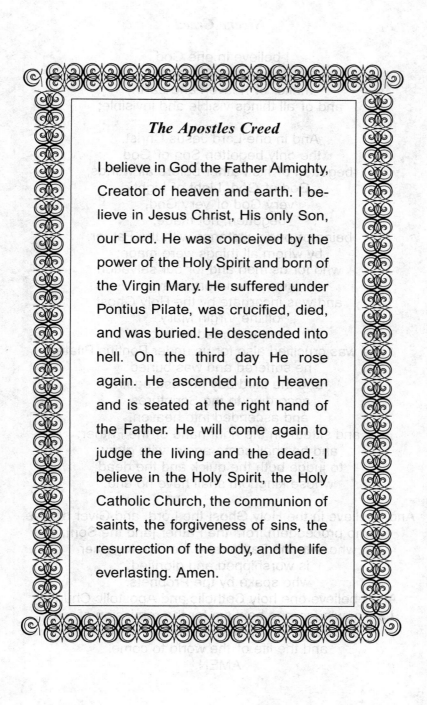

The Apostles Creed

I believe in God the Father Almighty, Creator of heaven and earth. I believe in Jesus Christ, His only Son, our Lord. He was conceived by the power of the Holy Spirit and born of the Virgin Mary. He suffered under Pontius Pilate, was crucified, died, and was buried. He descended into hell. On the third day He rose again. He ascended into Heaven and is seated at the right hand of the Father. He will come again to judge the living and the dead. I believe in the Holy Spirit, the Holy Catholic Church, the communion of saints, the forgiveness of sins, the resurrection of the body, and the life everlasting. Amen.

Nicene Creed

I believe in one God,
the Father Almighty,
maker of heaven and earth,
and of all things visible and invisible;

And in one Lord Jesus Christ,
the only begotten Son of God,
begotten of his Father before all worlds,
God of God, Light of Light,
very God of very God,
begotten, not made,
being of one substance with the Father;
by whom all things were made;
who for us men and for our salvation
came down from heaven,
and was incarnate by the Holy Ghost
of the Virgin Mary,
and was made man;
and was crucified also for us under Pontius Pilate;
he suffered and was buried;
and the third day he rose again
according to the Scriptures,
and ascended into heaven,
and sitteth on the right hand of the Father;
and he shall come again, with glory,
to judge both the quick and the dead;
whose kingdom shall have no end.

And I believe in the Holy Ghost the Lord, and Giver of Live,
who proceedeth from the Father [and the Son];
who with the Father and the Son together
is worshipped and glorified;
who spake by the Prophets.
And I believe one holy Catholic and Apostolic Church;
I acknowledge one baptism for the remission of sins;
and I look for the resurrection of the dead,
and the life of the world to come.
AMEN.

Preface

In September 1966 the American Bible Society published *The New Testament in Today's English Version*, the first publication of a new Bible translation intended for people everywhere for whom English is either their mother tongue or an acquired language. Shortly thereafter the United Bible Societies (UBS) requested the American Bible Society (ABS) to undertake on its behalf a translation of the Old Testament following the same principles. Accordingly the American Bible Society appointed a group of translators to prepare the translation. In 1971 this group added a British consultant recommended by the British and Foreign Bible Society. The translation of the Old Testament, which was completed in 1976, was joined to the fourth edition New Testament, thus completing the first edition of the Good News Translation. Though previously known as Today's English Version (TEV) and commonly known as the Good News Bible (GNB), the translation is now called the Good News Translation (GNT).

Two ways to present the deuterocanonical books

The translation of the deuterocanonical books and others classed as Apocrypha was completed in 1978, and the first edition of the *Good News Translation* with Deuterocanonicals and Apocrypha was published in 1979, with the Imprimatur of the Most Reverend John F. Whealon, Archbishop of Hartford, Connecticut. The 1979 publication was an interconfessional edition in which these books were grouped in a separate section between the Old and the New Testaments.

In this present edition the deuterocanonical books are arranged in the order most familiar to Roman Catholics. The books of Tobit, Judith, and 1 and 2 Maccabees follow after the historical books Ezra and Nehemiah. The Book of Esther with its six additions follows Judith in this grouping. Most of these books were written or have their settings in the last several centuries B.C. The Book of Baruch, which in this edition incorporates the letter of Jeremiah, is positioned after Lamentations, as part of the Jeremiah grouping. The books of The Wisdom of Solomon and Sirach, being wisdom books, are located among the other Old Testament Wisdom books, immediately following Song of Songs. The three additions to the book of Daniel, which are presented as separate books in the interconfessional edition of the GNT, are presented here in the way most familiar to Roman Catholics. Susanna and Bel and the Dragon are traditionally treated as chapters B and C of Daniel. The third addition has its location between verses 23 and 24 of chapter 3 in the Hebrew text because this is the position it holds in the Septuagint. Known as the Prayer of Azariah and the Song of the Three Young Men, this addition to Daniel provides the text of the prayer offered by Azariah and of the song he and his companions sang while in the midst of the flames in the fiery furnace. The result is an Old Testament with forty-six books, several of which contain significant additions. These books formed part of the Septuagint, the Greek translation of the Old Testament that was in circulation at the time of Christ.

The text used for this translation

The basic Hebrew (and Aramaic) text for the Old Testament is the Masoretic Text made available through printed editions, published by the UBS, and since 1977 under the title of *Biblia Hebraica Stuttgartensia*. In some instances the words of the printed consonantal text have been divided differently or have been read with a different set of vowels; at times a variant reading in the margin of the Hebrew text (*qere*) has been followed instead of the reading in the text (*kethiv*); and in other instances a variant reading supported by one or more Hebrew manuscripts has been adopted. Where no Hebrew source yields a satisfactory meaning in the context, the translation has either followed one or more of the ancient versions (e.g. Greek, Syriac, Latin) or has adopted a reconstructed text (technically referred to as a conjectural emendation) based on scholarly consensus; such departures from the Hebrew are indicated in footnotes.

The basic text for the deuterocanonical books is the Greek text printed in the Septuagint (3rd edition, 1949), edited by Alfred Rahlfs. For some of these books the more recently published Goettingen edition of the Septuagint has also been consulted.

The basic text for the translation of the New Testament is *The Greek New Testament* published by the UBS (3rd edition, 1975), but in a few instances the translation is based on a variant reading supported by one or more Greek manuscripts.

The translation process

Drafts of the translation in its early stages were sent for comments and suggestions to a review panel consisting of prominent theologians and biblical scholars appointed by the American Bible Society Board of Managers in its capacity as trustee for the translation. In addition, drafts were sent to major English-speaking Bible Societies throughout the world. Final approval of the translation on behalf of the United Bible Societies was given by the American Bible Society's Board of Managers upon recommendation of its Translations Committee.

The primary concern of the translators was to provide a faithful translation of the meaning of the Hebrew, Aramaic, and Greek texts. Their first task was to understand correctly the meaning of the original. At times the original meaning cannot be precisely known, not only because the meaning of some words and phrases cannot be determined with a great degree of assurance, but also because the underlying cultural and historical context is sometimes beyond recovery. All aids available were used in this task, including the ancient versions and the modern translations in English and other languages. After ascertaining as accurately as possible the meaning of the original, the translators' next task was to express that meaning in a manner and form easily understood by the readers. Since this translation is intended for all who use English as a means of communication, the translators have tried to avoid words and forms not in current or widespread use; but no artificial limit has been set to the range of the vocabulary employed. Every effort has been made to use language that is natural, clear, simple, and unambiguous. Consequently there has been no attempt to reproduce in English the parts of speech, sentence structure, word order, and grammatical devices of the original languages. Faithfulness in translation also includes a faithful representation of the cultural and historical features of the original. Certain features, however, such as the hours of the day and the measures of weight, capacity, distance, and area, are given their modern equivalents, since the information in those terms conveys more meaning to the reader than the biblical form of those terms.

In cases where a person or place is called by two or more different names in the original, this translation has normally used only the more familiar name in all places; e.g. King Jehoiachin of Judah (Jeremiah 52.31), also called Jeconiah (Jeremiah 24.1) and Coniah (Jeremiah 37.1). Where a proper name is spelled two or more different ways in the original text, this translation has used only one spelling; e.g. Nebuchadnezzar, also spelled Nebuchadrezzar (Jeremiah 29.3 and 29.21), and Priscilla, also spelled Prisca (Acts 18.26 and Romans 16.3).

In view of the differences in vocabulary and form that exist between the American and the British use of the English language, a British edition of the GNT has been published, which incorporates changes that are in keeping with British usage.

Following an ancient tradition begun by the first translation of the Hebrew Scriptures into Greek (the Septuagint) and followed by the vast majority of English translations, the distinctive Hebrew name for God (usually transliterated *Jehovah* or *Yahweh*) is in this translation represented by "LORD." When *Adonai*, normally translated "Lord," is followed by *Yahweh*, the combination is rendered by the phrase "Sovereign LORD."

The revision of the Good News Translation

Since the initial appearance of the full GNT Bible in 1976, some minor editorial changes and corrections of printing errors have been introduced into the text in connection with various printings. The New Testament was already in its fourth edition at the time the full Bible appeared, but for the Old Testament and the Deuterocanonicals/Apocrypha of the GNT there was no revised edition until 1992. The preparation and publication of the second edition of the full GNT Bible in two formats, with and without the Deuterocanonicals and Apocrypha, is the result of a broad international process of careful review and evaluation of the GNT translation by many scholars and experts over a period of several years.

In December l986, acting in response to a mounting perception of a need for text revisions, the ABS Board of Managers approved the undertaking of a revision of the GNT translation. The revision was restricted to two main areas of concern that had been raised and discussed over the years since the first appearance of the translation: (1) passages in which the English style had been unnecessarily exclusive and inattentive to gender concerns, and (2) passages in which the translation had been seen as problematic from either a stylistic or an exegetical viewpoint.

The process followed in preparing this revised edition was one of first inviting and collecting proposals for needed revisions from all English-language Bible Societies and English-speaking UBS translations consultants around the world, as well as numerous scholarly consultants in the United States and representatives of various American churches. The proposals received were then assembled for review and evaluation by the same broad array of experts whose specializations included translation, linguistics, English usage, literary and poetic style, biblical studies, and theology. In a series of four stages, consensus was sought on which proposals were necessary and valid, and at each of these review stages the number of proposals under consideration was reduced until widespread agreement was reached. On the recommendation of the program committee of the ABS Board of Trustees, and its translations subcommittee, the ABS Board acted to approve the revisions for the Good News Second Edition. These revisions have also incorporated for use in British usage editions of the GNT.

In the decade and a half since the initial publication of the full GNT Bible, many Bible readers had become sensitive to the negative effects of exclusive language; that is, to the ways in which the built-in linguistic biases of the ancient languages and the English language toward the masculine gender has led some Bible readers to feel excluded from being addressed by the scriptural Word. This concern has led to the revision of most major English translations during the l980s, and, increasingly, readers of the GNT wrote to request that the Bible Society take this concern into consideration in preparing any revision. In practical terms what this means is that, where references in particular passages are to both men and women, the revision aims at language that is not exclusively masculine-oriented. At the same time, however, great care was taken not to distort the historical reality of the ancient patriarchal culture of Bible times.

Helps for the reader

In order to make the text easier to understand, various kinds of readers' helps are supplied. The text itself has been divided into sections, and headings are provided which indicate the contents of the section. Where there are parallel accounts elsewhere in the Bible, as happens frequently in the Gospels, a reference to such a passage appears within parentheses below the heading. There are, in addition, several kinds of notes which appear at the bottom of the page. (1) *Cultural or Historical Notes.* These provide information required to enable the reader to understand the meaning of the text in terms of its original setting (e.g. the explanation of *Rahab* in Psalm 89.10; the explanation of *Day of Atonement* in Acts 27.9). (2) *Textual Notes.* In the Old Testament these indicate primarily those places where the translators were compelled for a variety of reasons to base the translation on some text other than the Hebrew. Where one or more of the ancient versions were followed, the note indicates this by *One ancient translation* (e.g. Genesis 1.26) or *Some ancient translations* (e.g. Genesis 4.8); where a conjectural emendation was adopted, the note reads *Probable text* (e.g. Genesis 10.14). In the New Testament, as well as in the deuterocanonicals, there are textual notes indicating some of the places where there are significant differences among the ancient manuscripts. These differences may consist of additions to the text (e.g. Matthew 21.43), deletions (e.g. Matthew 24.36), or substitutions (e.g. Mark 1.41). (3) *Alternative Renderings*. In many places the precise meaning of the original text is in dispute, and there are two or more different ways in which the text may be understood. In some of the more important of such instances an alternative rendering is given (e.g. Genesis 2.9; Matthew 6.11). (4) *References to Other Passages*. In addition, many editions of the Good News Bible include references, (by book, chapter, and verse) to other places in the Bible where identical or similar matters or ideas are dealt with.

There are several appendices at the end of the volume. A *Word List* identifies many objects or cultural features whose meaning may not be known to all readers. A List of *New Testament Passages Quoted or Paraphrased from the Septuagint* (the ancient Greek translation of the Old Testament) identifies those passages which differ significantly in meaning from the Hebrew Masoretic Text. This list should help readers understand some otherwise puzzling differences in quotations. The *Chronology of the Bible* is a chart that gives the approximate dates of the major events recorded in the Bible. The *Maps* are designed to help the reader to visualize the geographical setting of countries and localities mentioned in the Bible at different points in their history. A *Subject Index* locates by biblical reference some of the more important subjects, persons, places, and events in the Bible.

The line drawings that accompany the text were specially prepared for this translation.

The numbering of chapters and verses in this translation follows the traditional system of major English translations of the Bible. In some instances, however, where the order of thought or events in two or more verses is more clearly represented by a rearrangement of the material, two or more verse numbers are joined (e.g. Exodus 2.15–16; Acts 1.21–22).

A Bible that brings good news

No one knows better than the translators how difficult their task has been. But they performed it gladly, conscious always of the presence of the Holy Spirit and of the tremendous debt that they owe to the dedication and scholarship of those who have preceded them. The Bible is not simply great literature to be admired and revered; it is Good News for all people everywhere—a message both to be understood and to be applied in daily life. It is with prayer and thankfulness that the translator and staff of the United Bible Societies and American Bible Society offer this translation to the Lord; it is with humility that we pray God will make it fruitful. And to Christ be the glory forever and ever!

Old Testament

The Garden of Eden

When the LORDᵃ God made the universe, ⁵there were no plants on the earth and no seeds had sprouted, because he had not sent any rain, and there was no one to cultivate the land; ⁶but water would come up from beneath the surface and water the ground.

⁷Then the LORD God took some soil from the groundᵇ and formed a manᵇ out of it; he breathed life-giving breath into his nostrils and the man began to live.

⁸Then the LORD God planted a garden in Eden, in the East, and there he put the man he had formed. ⁹He made all kinds of beautiful trees grow there and produce good fruit. In the middle of the garden stood the tree that gives life and the tree that gives knowledge of what is good and what is bad.ᶜ

¹⁰A stream flowed in Eden and watered the garden; beyond Eden it divided into four rivers. ¹¹The first river is the Pishon; it flows around the country of Havilah. (¹²Pure gold is found there and also rare perfume and precious stones.) ¹³The second river is the Gihon; it flows around the country of Cush.ᵈ ¹⁴The third river is the Tigris, which flows east of Assyria, and the fourth river is the Euphrates.

¹⁵Then the LORD God placed the man in the Garden of Eden to cultivate it and guard it. ¹⁶He told him, "You may eat the fruit of any tree in the garden, ¹⁷except the tree that gives knowledge of what is good and what is bad.ᶜ You must not eat the fruit of that tree; if you do, you will die the same day."

¹⁸Then the LORD God said, "It is not good for the man to live alone. I will make a suitable companion to help him." ¹⁹So he took some soil from the ground and formed all the animals and all the birds. Then he brought them to the man to see what he would name them; and that is how they all got their names. ²⁰So the man named all the birds and all the animals; but not one of them was a suitable companion to help him.

²¹Then the LORD God made the man fall into a deep sleep, and while he was sleeping, he took out one of the man's ribs and closed up the flesh. ²²He formed a woman out of the rib and brought her to him. ²³Then the man said,

"At last, here is one of my own kind—
Bone taken from my bone, and flesh from my flesh.
'Woman' is her name because she was taken out of man."ᵉ

²⁴That is why a man leaves his father and mother and is united with his wife, and they become one.

²⁵The man and the woman were both naked, but they were not embarrassed.

Human Disobedience

3 Now the snake was the most cunning animal that the LORD God had made. The snake asked the woman, "Did God really tell you not to eat fruit from any tree in the garden?"

²"We may eat the fruit of any tree in the garden," the woman answered, ³"except the tree in the middle of it. God told us not to eat the fruit of that tree or even touch it; if we do, we will die."

⁴The snake replied, "That's not true; you will not die. ⁵God said that because he knows that when you eat it, you will be like Godᶠ and know what is good and what is bad."ᵍ

⁶The woman saw how beautiful the tree was and how good its fruit would be to eat, and she thought how wonderful it would be to become wise. So she took some of the

How wonderful it would be to become wise! (3.6)

ᵃTHE LORD: *Where the Hebrew text has Yahweh, traditionally transliterated as Jehovah, this translation employs* LORD *with capital letters, following a usage which is widespread in English versions.* ᵇGROUND . . . MAN: *The Hebrew words for "man" and "ground" have similar sounds.* ᶜknowledge of what is good and what is bad; *or* knowledge of everything. ᵈCUSH: *Usually means Ethiopia, but here may refer to a place in Mesopotamia.* ᵉWOMAN . . . MAN: *The Hebrew words for "woman" and "man" have rather similar sounds.* ᶠGod; *or* the gods. ᵍknow what is good and what is bad; *or* know everything.

2.7 Ws 15.8, 11; 1 Co 15.45   **2.9** Rev 2.7; 22.2, 14   **2.24** Mt 19.5; Mk 10.7, 8; 1 Co 6.16; Eph 5.31
3.1 Ws 2.24; Rev 12.9; 20.2

fruit and ate it. Then she gave some to her husband, and he also ate it. ⁷As soon as they had eaten it, they were given understanding and realized that they were naked; so they sewed fig leaves together and covered themselves.

⁸That evening they heard the LORD God walking in the garden, and they hid from him among the trees. ⁹But the LORD God called out to the man, "Where are you?"

¹⁰He answered, "I heard you in the garden; I was afraid and hid from you, because I was naked."

¹¹"Who told you that you were naked?" God asked. "Did you eat the fruit that I told you not to eat?"

¹²The man answered, "The woman you put here with me gave me the fruit, and I ate it."

¹³The LORD God asked the woman, "Why did you do this?"

She replied, "The snake tricked me into eating it."

God Pronounces Judgment

¹⁴Then the LORD God said to the snake, "You will be punished for this; you alone of all the animals must bear this curse: From now on you will crawl on your belly, and you will have to eat dust as long as you live. ¹⁵I will make you and the woman hate each other; her offspring and yours will always be enemies. Her offspring will crush your head, and you will bite her offspring's*a* heel."

¹⁶And he said to the woman, "I will increase your trouble in pregnancy and your pain in giving birth. In spite of this, you will still have desire for your husband, yet you will be subject to him."

¹⁷And he said to the man, "You listened to your wife and ate the fruit which I told you not to eat. Because of what you have done, the ground will be under a curse. You will have to work hard all your life to make it produce enough food for you. ¹⁸It will produce weeds and thorns, and you will have to eat wild plants. ¹⁹You will have to work hard and sweat to make the soil produce anything, until you go back to the soil from which you were formed. You were made from soil, and you will become soil again."

²⁰Adam*b* named his wife Eve,*c* because she was the mother of all human beings. ²¹And the LORD God made clothes out of animal skins for Adam and his wife, and he clothed them.

Adam and Eve Are Sent Out of the Garden

²²Then the LORD God said, "Now these human beings have become like one of us and have knowledge of what is good and what is bad.*d* They must not be allowed to take fruit from the tree that gives life, eat it, and live forever." ²³So the LORD God sent them out of the Garden of Eden and made them cultivate the soil from which they had been formed. ²⁴Then at the east side of the garden he put living creatures*e* and a flaming sword which turned in all directions. This was to keep anyone from coming near the tree that gives life.

Cain and Abel

4 Then Adam had intercourse with his wife, and she became pregnant. She bore a son and said, "By the LORD's help I have gotten a son." So she named him Cain.*f* ²Later she gave birth to another son, Abel. Abel became a shepherd, but Cain was a farmer. ³After some time Cain brought some of his harvest and gave it as an offering to the LORD. ⁴Then Abel brought the first lamb born to one of his sheep, killed it, and gave the best parts of it as an offering. The LORD was pleased with Abel and his offering, ⁵but he rejected Cain and his offering. Cain became furious, and he scowled in anger. ⁶Then the LORD said to Cain, "Why are you angry? Why that scowl on your face? ⁷If you had done the right thing, you would be smiling;*g* but because you have done evil, sin is crouching at your door. It wants to rule you, but you must overcome it."

---

*a*her offspring's; or their.   *b*ADAM: *This name in Hebrew means "all human beings."*   *c*EVE: *This name sounds similar to the Hebrew word for "living," which is rendered in this context as "human beings."*
*d*knowledge of what is good and what is bad; or knowledge of everything.   *e*LIVING CREATURES: *See Word List.*
*f*CAIN: *This name sounds like the Hebrew for "gotten."*   *g*you would be smiling; or I would have accepted your offering.

3.13 2 Co 11.3; 1 Ti 2.14   **3.15** Rev 12.17   **3.17, 18** He 6.8   **3.22** Rev 22.14   **4.4** He 11.4

[8]Then Cain said to his brother Abel, "Let's go out in the fields."[a] When they were out in the fields, Cain turned on his brother and killed him.

[9]The LORD asked Cain, "Where is your brother Abel?"

He answered, "I don't know. Am I supposed to take care of my brother?"

[10]Then the LORD said, "Why have you done this terrible thing? Your brother's blood is crying out to me from the ground, like a voice calling for revenge. [11]You are placed under a curse and can no longer farm the soil. It has soaked up your brother's blood as if it had opened its mouth to receive it when you killed him. [12]If you try to grow crops, the soil will not produce anything; you will be a homeless wanderer on the earth."

[13]And Cain said to the LORD, "This punishment is too hard for me to bear. [14]You are driving me off the land and away from your presence. I will be a homeless wanderer on the earth, and anyone who finds me will kill me."

"Why that scowl on your face?" (4.6)

[15]But the LORD answered, "No. If anyone kills you, seven lives will be taken in revenge." So the LORD put a mark on Cain to warn anyone who met him not to kill him. [16]And Cain went away from the LORD's presence and lived in a land called "Wandering," which is east of Eden.

The Descendants of Cain

[17]Cain and his wife had a son and named him Enoch. Then Cain built a city and named it after his son. [18]Enoch had a son named Irad, who was the father of Mehujael, and Mehujael had a son named Methushael, who was the father of Lamech. [19]Lamech had two wives, Adah and Zillah. [20]Adah gave birth to Jabal, who was the ancestor of those who raise livestock and live in tents. [21]His brother was Jubal, the ancestor of all musicians who play the harp and the flute. [22]Zillah gave birth to Tubal Cain, who made all kinds of tools out of bronze and iron.[b] The sister of Tubal Cain was Naamah.

[23]Lamech said to his wives,

"Adah and Zillah, listen to me:
I have killed a young man because he struck me.
[24]If seven lives are taken to pay for killing Cain,
Seventy-seven will be taken if anyone kills me."

Seth and Enosh

[25]Adam and his wife had another son. She said, "God has given me a son to replace Abel, whom Cain killed." So she named him Seth.[c] [26]Seth had a son whom he named Enosh. It was then that people began using the LORD's holy name in worship.

The Descendants of Adam
(1 Chronicles 1.1-4)

5 This is the list of the descendants of Adam. (When God created human beings, he made them like himself. [2]He created them male and female, blessed them, and named them "Human Beings.") [3]When Adam was 130 years old, he had a son who was like him, and he named him Seth. [4]After that, Adam lived another 800 years. He had other children [5]and died at the age of 930.

---

[a]*Some ancient translations* Let's go out in the fields; *Hebrew does not have these words.*   [b]who made all kinds of tools out of bronze and iron; *one ancient translation* who was the ancestor of all metalworkers.
[c]SETH: *This name sounds like the Hebrew for "has given."*
4.8 Ws 10.3; Mt 23.35; Lk 11.51; 1 Jn 3.12   **4.10** He 12.24   **5.1, 2** Gn 1.27, 28   **5.2** Mt 19.4; Mk 10.6

⁶When Seth was 105, he had a son, Enosh, ⁷and then lived another 807 years. He had other children ⁸and died at the age of 912.

⁹When Enosh was 90, he had a son, Kenan, ¹⁰and then lived another 815 years. He had other children ¹¹and died at the age of 905.

¹²When Kenan was 70, he had a son, Mahalalel, ¹³and then lived another 840 years. He had other children ¹⁴and died at the age of 910.

¹⁵When Mahalalel was 65, he had a son, Jared, ¹⁶and then lived another 830 years. He had other children ¹⁷and died at the age of 895.

¹⁸When Jared was 162, he had a son, Enoch, ¹⁹and then lived another 800 years. He had other children ²⁰and died at the age of 962.

²¹When Enoch was 65, he had a son, Methuselah. ²²After that, Enoch lived in fellowship with God for 300 years and had other children. ²³He lived to be 365 years old. ²⁴He spent his life in fellowship with God, and then he disappeared, because God took him away.

²⁵When Methuselah was 187, he had a son, Lamech, ²⁶and then lived another 782 years. He had other children ²⁷and died at the age of 969.

²⁸When Lamech was 182, he had a son ²⁹and said, "From the very ground on which the LORD put a curse, this child will bring us relief from all our hard work"; so he named him Noah.ᵃ ³⁰Lamech lived another 595 years. He had other children ³¹and died at the age of 777.

³²After Noah was 500 years old, he had three sons, Shem, Ham, and Japheth.

Human Wickedness

6 When people had spread all over the world, and daughters were being born, ²some of the heavenly beingsᵇ saw that these young women were beautiful, so they took the ones they liked. ³Then the LORD said, "I will not allow people to live forever; they are mortal. From now on they will live no longer than 120 years. ⁴In those days, and even later, there were giants on the earth who were descendants of human women and the heavenly beings. They were the great heroes and famous men of long ago.

⁵When the LORD saw how wicked everyone on earth was and how evil their thoughts were all the time, ⁶he was sorry that he had ever made them and put them on the earth. He was so filled with regret ⁷that he said, "I will wipe out these people I have created, and also the animals and the birds, because I am sorry that I made any of them." ⁸But the LORD was pleased with Noah.

Noah

⁹⁻¹⁰This is the story of Noah. He had three sons, Shem, Ham, and Japheth. Noah had no faults and was the only good man of his time. He lived in fellowship with God, ¹¹but everyone else was evil in God's sight, and violence had spread everywhere. ¹²God looked at the world and saw that it was evil, for the people were all living evil lives.

¹³God said to Noah, "I have decided to put an end to all people. I will destroy them completely, because the world is full of their violent deeds. ¹⁴Build a boat for yourself out of good timber; make rooms in it and cover it with tar inside and out. ¹⁵Make it 450 feet long, 75 feet wide, and 45 feet high. ¹⁶Make a roofᶜ for the boat and leave a space of 18 inches between the roofᶜ and the sides. Build it with three decks and put a door in the side. ¹⁷I am going to send a flood on the earth to destroy every living being. Everything on the earth will die, ¹⁸but I will make a covenant with you. Go into the boat with your wife, your sons, and their wives. ¹⁹⁻²⁰Take into the boat with you a male and a female of every kind of animal and of every kind of bird, in order to keep them alive. ²¹Take along all kinds of food for you and for them." ²² Noah did everything that God commanded.

The Flood

7 The LORD said to Noah, "Go into the boat with your whole family; I have found that you are the only one in all the world who does what is right. ²Take with you seven pairs of each kind of ritually clean animal, but only one pair of each kind of unclean animal. ³Take

---

ᵃNOAH: *This name sounds like the Hebrew for "relief."*   ᵇheavenly beings; *or* sons of the gods; *or* sons of God.   ᶜroof; *or* window.
5.24 Si 44.16; 49.14; He 11.5; Jd 14   **6.1-4** Job 1.6; 2.1   **6.4** Nu 13.33; Si 16.7; Ba 3.26   **6.5-8** Mt 24.37; Lk 17.26; 1 P 3.20   **6.9** Si 44.17, 18; 2 P 2.5   **6.22** He 11.7

also seven pairs of each kind of bird. Do this so that every kind of animal and bird will be kept alive to reproduce again on the earth. ⁴Seven days from now I am going to send rain that will fall for forty days and nights, in order to destroy all the living beings that I have made." ⁵And Noah did everything that the LORD commanded.

⁶Noah was six hundred years old when the flood came on the earth. ⁷He and his wife, and his sons and their wives, went into the boat to escape the flood. ⁸A male and a female of every kind of animal and bird, whether ritually clean or unclean, ⁹went into the boat with Noah, as God had commanded. ¹⁰Seven days later the flood came.

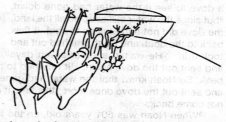

¹¹When Noah was six hundred years old, on the seventeenth day of the second month all the outlets of the vast body of water beneath the earth burst open, all the floodgates of the sky were opened, ¹²and rain fell on the earth for forty days and nights. ¹³On that same day Noah and his wife went into the boat with their three sons, Shem, Ham, and Japheth, and their wives. ¹⁴With them went every kind of animal, domestic and wild, large and small, and every kind of bird. ¹⁵A male and a female of each kind of living being went into the boat with Noah, ¹⁶as God had commanded. Then the LORD shut the door behind Noah.

¹⁷The flood continued for forty days, and the water became deep enough for the boat to float. ¹⁸The water became deeper, and the boat drifted on the surface. ¹⁹It became so deep that it covered the highest mountains; ²⁰it went on rising until it was about twenty-five feet above the tops of the mountains. ²¹Every living being on the earth died—every bird, every animal, and every person. ²²Everything on earth that breathed died. ²³The LORD destroyed all living beings on the earth—human beings, animals, and birds. The only ones left were Noah and those who were with him in the boat. ²⁴The water did not start going down for a hundred and fifty days.

The End of the Flood

8 God had not forgotten Noah and all the animals with him in the boat; he caused a wind to blow, and the water started going down. ²The outlets of the water beneath the earth and the floodgates of the sky were closed. The rain stopped, ³and the water gradually went down for 150 days. ⁴On the seventeenth day of the seventh month the boat came to rest on a moun-

7.7 Mt 24.38, 39; Lk 17.27   **7.11** 2 P 3.6

Every kind of animal and bird . . . went into the boat. (7.8,9)

tain in the Ararat range. ⁵The water kept going down, and on the first day of the tenth month the tops of the mountains appeared.

⁶After forty days Noah opened a window ⁷and sent out a raven. It did not come back, but kept flying around until the water was completely gone. ⁸Meanwhile, Noah sent out a dove to see if the water had gone down, ⁹but since the water still covered all the land, the dove did not find a place to light. It flew back to the boat, and Noah reached out and took it in. ¹⁰He waited another seven days

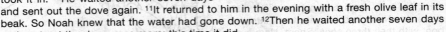

Everything on earth that breathed died. (7.22)

and sent out the dove again. ¹¹It returned to him in the evening with a fresh olive leaf in its beak. So Noah knew that the water had gone down. ¹²Then he waited another seven days and sent out the dove once more; this time it did not come back.

¹³When Noah was 601 years old, on the first day of the first month, the water was gone. Noah removed the covering of the boat, looked around, and saw that the ground was getting dry. ¹⁴By the twenty-seventh day of the second month the earth was completely dry.

¹⁵God said to Noah, ¹⁶"Go out of the boat with your wife, your sons, and their wives. ¹⁷Take all the birds and animals out with you, so that they may reproduce and spread over all the earth." ¹⁸So

The water had gone down. (8.11)

Noah went out of the boat with his wife, his sons, and their wives. ¹⁹All the animals and birds went out of the boat in groups of their own kind.

Noah Offers a Sacrifice

²⁰Noah built an altar to the LORD; he took one of each kind of ritually clean animal and bird, and burned them whole as a sacrifice on the altar. ²¹The odor of the sacrifice pleased the LORD, and he said to himself, "Never again will I put the earth under a curse because of what people do; I know that from the time they are young their thoughts are evil. Never again will I destroy all living beings, as I have done this time. ²²As long as the world exists, there will be a time for planting and a time for harvest. There will always be cold and heat, summer and winter, day and night."

God's Covenant with Noah

9 God blessed Noah and his sons and said, "Have many children, so that your descendants will live all over the earth. ²All the animals, birds, and fish will live in fear of you. They are all placed under your power. ³Now you can eat them, as well as green plants; I give them all to you for food. ⁴The one thing you must not eat is meat with blood still in it; I forbid this because the life is in the blood. ⁵If anyone takes human life, he will be punished. I will punish with death any animal that takes a human life. ⁶Human beings were made like God, so whoever murders one of them will be killed by someone else.

⁷"You must have many children, so that your descendants will live all over the earth."

⁸God said to Noah and his sons, ⁹"I am now making my covenant with you and with your descendants, ¹⁰and with all living beings—all birds and all animals—everything that came out of the boat with you. ¹¹With these words I make my covenant with you: I promise that never again will all living beings be destroyed by a flood; never again will a flood destroy the earth. ¹²As a sign of this everlasting covenant which I am making with you and with all living beings, ¹³I am putting my bow in the clouds. It will be the sign of my covenant with the world. ¹⁴Whenever I cover the sky with clouds and the rainbow appears, ¹⁵I will remember

9.1 Gn 1.28 **9.4** Lv 7.26, 27; 17.10-14; 19.26; Dt 12.16, 23; 15.23 **9.6** Ex 20.13; Gn 1.26
9.7 Gn 1.28

The sign of my covenant with the world (9.13)

my promise to you and to all the animals that a flood will never again destroy all living beings. ¹⁶When the rainbow appears in the clouds, I will see it and remember the everlasting covenant between me and all living beings on earth. ¹⁷That is the sign of the promise which I am making to all living beings."

Noah and His Sons

¹⁸The sons of Noah who went out of the boat were Shem, Ham, and Japheth. (Ham was the father of Canaan.) ¹⁹These three sons of Noah were the ancestors of all the people on earth.

²⁰Noah, who was a farmer, was the first man to plant a vineyard. ²¹After he drank some of the wine, he became drunk, took off his clothes, and lay naked in his tent. ²²When Ham, the father of Canaan, saw that his father was naked, he went out and told his two brothers. ²³Then Shem and Japheth took a robe and held it behind them on their shoulders. They walked backward into the tent and covered their father, keeping their faces turned away so as not to see him naked. ²⁴When Noah sobered up and learned what his youngest son had done to him, ²⁵he said,

"A curse on Canaan!
He will be a slave to his brothers.
²⁶Give praise to the LORD, the God of Shem!
Canaan will be the slave of Shem.
²⁷May God cause Japheth[a] to increase!
May his descendants live with the people of Shem!
Canaan will be the slave of Japheth."

²⁸After the flood Noah lived 350 years ²⁹and died at the age of 950.

The Descendants of Noah's Sons

(1 Chronicles 1.5-23)

10 These are the descendants of Noah's sons, Shem, Ham, and Japheth. These three had sons after the flood.

²The sons of Japheth—Gomer, Magog, Madai, Javan, Tubal, Meshech, and Tiras—were the ancestors of the peoples who bear their names. ³The descendants of Gomer were the

[a]JAPHETH: *This name sounds like the Hebrew for "increase."*

people of Ashkenaz, Riphath, and Togarmah. ⁴The descendants of Javan were the people of Elishah, Spain, Cyprus, and Rhodes; ⁵they were the ancestors of the people who live along the coast and on the islands. These are the descendants of Japheth, living in their different tribes and countries, each group speaking its own language.

⁶The sons of Ham—Cush, Egypt, Libya, and Canaan—were the ancestors of the peoples who bear their names. ⁷The descendants of Cush were the people of Seba, Havilah, Sabtah, Raamah, and Sabteca. The descendants of Raamah were the people of Sheba and Dedan. ⁸Cush had a son named Nimrod, who became the world's first great conqueror. ⁹By the LORD's help he was a great hunter, and that is why people say, "May the LORD make you as great a hunter as Nimrod!" ¹⁰At first his kingdom included Babylon, Erech, and Accad, all three of them in Babylonia. ¹¹From that land he went to Assyria and built the cities of Nineveh, Rehoboth Ir, Calah, ¹²and Resen, which is between Nineveh and the great city of Calah.

¹³The descendants of Egypt were the people of Lydia, Anam, Lehab, Naphtuh, ¹⁴Pathrus, Casluh, and of Crete, from whom the Philistines are descended.ᵃ

¹⁵Canaan's sons—Sidon, the oldest, and Heth—were the ancestors of the peoples who bear their names. ¹⁶Canaan was also the ancestor of the Jebusites, the Amorites, the Girgashites, ¹⁷the Hivites, the Arkites, the Sinites, ¹⁸the Arvadites, the Zemarites, and the Hamathites. The different tribes of the Canaanites spread out, ¹⁹until the Canaanite borders reached from Sidon southward to Gerar near Gaza, and eastward to Sodom, Gomorrah, Admah, and Zeboiim near Lasha. ²⁰These are the descendants of Ham, living in their different tribes and countries, each group speaking its own language.

²¹Shem, the older brother of Japheth, was the ancestor of all the Hebrews. ²²Shem's sons—Elam, Asshur, Arpachshad, Lud, and Aram—were the ancestors of the peoples who bear their names. ²³The descendants of Aram were the people of Uz, Hul, Gether, and Meshek. ²⁴Arpachshad was the father of Shelah, who was the father of Eber. ²⁵Eber had two sons: one was named Peleg,ᵇ because during his time the people of the world were divided; and the other was named Joktan. ²⁶The descendants of Joktan were the people of Almodad, Sheleph, Hazarmaveth, Jerah, ²⁷Hadoram, Uzal, Diklah, ²⁸Obal, Abimael, Sheba, ²⁹Ophir, Havilah, and Jobab. All of them were descended from Joktan. ³⁰The land in which they lived extended from Mesha to Sephar in the eastern hill country. ³¹These are the descendants of Shem, living in their different tribes and countries, each group speaking its own language.

³²All these peoples are the descendants of Noah, nation by nation, according to their different lines of descent. After the flood all the nations of the earth were descended from the sons of Noah.

The Tower of Babylon

11 At first, the people of the whole world had only one language and used the same words. ²As they wandered about in the East, they came to a plain in Babylonia and settled there. ³They said to one another, "Come on! Let's make bricks and bake them hard." So they had bricks to build with and tar to hold them together. ⁴They said, "Now let's build a city with a tower that reaches the sky, so that we can make a name for ourselves and not be scattered all over the earth."

⁵Then the LORD came down to see the city and the tower which they had built, ⁶and he said, "Now then, these are all one people and they speak one language; this is just the beginning of what they are going to do. Soon they will be able to do anything they want! ⁷Let us go down and mix up their language so that they will not understand each other." ⁸So the LORD scattered them all over the earth, and they stopped building the city. ⁹The city was called Babylon,ᶜ because there the LORD mixed up the language of all the people, and from there he scattered them all over the earth.

The Descendants of Shem
(1 Chronicles 1.24-27)

¹⁰These are the descendants of Shem. Two years after the flood, when Shem was 100 years old, he had a son, Arpachshad. ¹¹After that, he lived another 500 years and had other children.

ᵃProbable text and of Crete . . . descended; Hebrew from whom the Philistines are descended, and Crete.
ᵇPELEG: This name sounds like the Hebrew for "divide." ᶜBABYLON: This name sounds like the Hebrew for "mixed up."

¹²When Arpachshad was 35 years old, he had a son, Shelah; ¹³after that, he lived another 403 years and had other children.

¹⁴When Shelah was 30 years old, he had a son, Eber; ¹⁵after that, he lived another 403 years and had other children.

¹⁶When Eber was 34 years old, he had a son, Peleg; ¹⁷after that, he lived another 430 years and had other children.

¹⁸When Peleg was 30 years old, he had a son, Reu; ¹⁹after that, he lived another 209 years and had other children.

²⁰When Reu was 32 years old, he had a son, Serug; ²¹after that, he lived another 207 years and had other children.

²²When Serug was 30 years old, he had a son, Nahor; ²³after that, he lived another 200 years and had other children.

²⁴When Nahor was 29 years old, he had a son, Terah; ²⁵after that, he lived another 119 years and had other children.

²⁶After Terah was 70 years old, he became the father of Abram, Nahor, and Haran.

The Descendants of Terah

²⁷These are the descendants of Terah, who was the father of Abram, Nahor, and Haran. Haran was the father of Lot, ²⁸and Haran died in his hometown of Ur in Babylonia, while his father was still living. ²⁹Abram married Sarai, and Nahor married Milcah, the daughter of Haran, who was also the father of Iscah. ³⁰Sarai was not able to have children.

³¹Terah took his son Abram, his grandson Lot, who was the son of Haran, and his daughter-in-law Sarai, Abram's wife, and with them he left the city of Ur in Babylonia to go to the land of Canaan. They went as far as Haran and settled there. ³²Terah died there at the age of 205.

God's Call to Abram

12 The LORD said to Abram, "Leave your country, your relatives, and your father's home, and go to a land that I am going to show you. ²I will give you many descendants, and they will become a great nation. I will bless you and make your name famous, so that you will be a blessing.

³I will bless those who bless you,
But I will curse those who curse you.
And through you I will bless all the nations."ᵃ

⁴When Abram was seventy-five years old, he started out from Haran, as the LORD had told him to do; and Lot went with him. ⁵Abram took his wife Sarai, his nephew Lot, and all the wealth and all the slaves they had acquired in Haran, and they started out for the land of Canaan.

When they arrived in Canaan, ⁶Abram traveled through the land until he came to the sacred tree of Moreh, the holy place at Shechem. (At that time the Canaanites were still living in the land.) ⁷The LORD appeared to Abram and said to him, "This is the country that I am going to give to your descendants." Then Abram built an altar there to the LORD, who had appeared to him. ⁸After that, he moved on south to the hill country east of the city of Bethel and set up his camp between Bethel on the west and Ai on the east. There also he built an altar and worshiped the LORD. ⁹Then he moved on from place to place, going toward the southern part of Canaan.

Abram in Egypt

¹⁰But there was a famine in Canaan, and it was so bad that Abram went farther south to Egypt, to live there for a while. ¹¹When he was about to cross the border into Egypt, he said to his wife Sarai, "You are a beautiful woman. ¹²When the Egyptians see you, they will assume that you are my wife, and so they will kill me and let you live. ¹³Tell them that you are my sister; then because of you they will let me live and treat me well." ¹⁴When he crossed the border into Egypt, the Egyptians did see that his wife was beautiful. ¹⁵Some of the court officials saw her and told the king how beautiful she was; so she was taken to his palace.

ᵃAnd through . . . nations; *or* All the nations will ask me to bless them as I have blessed you.
12.1 Ws 10.5; Ac 7.2, 3; He 11.8   **12.3** Ga 3.8   **12.7** Ac 7.5; Ga 3.16   **12.13** Gn 20.2; 26.7

¹⁶Because of her the king treated Abram well and gave him flocks of sheep and goats, cattle, donkeys, slaves, and camels.

¹⁷But because the king had taken Sarai, the LORD sent terrible diseases on him and on the people of his palace. ¹⁸Then the king sent for Abram and asked him, "What have you done to me? Why didn't you tell me that she was your wife? ¹⁹Why did you say that she was your sister, and let me take her as my wife? Here is your wife; take her and get out!" ²⁰The king gave orders to his men, so they took Abram and put him out of the country, together with his wife and everything he owned.

Abram and Lot Separate

13 Abram went north out of Egypt to the southern part of Canaan with his wife and everything he owned, and Lot went with him. ²Abram was a very rich man, with sheep, goats, and cattle, as well as silver and gold. ³Then he left there and moved from place to place, going toward Bethel. He reached the place between Bethel and Ai where he had camped before ⁴and had built an altar. There he worshiped the LORD.

⁵Lot also had sheep, goats, and cattle, as well as his own family and servants. ⁶And so there was not enough pasture land for the two of them to stay together, because they had too many animals. ⁷So quarrels broke out between the men who took care of Abram's animals and those who took care of Lot's animals. (At that time the Canaanites and the Perizzites were still living in the land.)

⁸Then Abram said to Lot, "We are relatives, and your men and my men shouldn't be quarreling. ⁹So let's separate. Choose any part of the land you want. You go one way, and I'll go the other."

¹⁰Lot looked around and saw that the whole Jordan Valley, all the way to Zoar, had plenty of water, like the Garden of the LORDᵃ or like the land of Egypt. (This was before the LORD had destroyed the cities of Sodom and Gomorrah.) ¹¹So Lot chose the whole Jordan Valley for himself and moved away toward the east. That is how the two men parted. ¹²Abram stayed in the land of Canaan, and Lot settled among the cities in the valley and camped near Sodom, ¹³whose people were wicked and sinned against the LORD.

Abram Moves to Hebron

¹⁴After Lot had left, the LORD said to Abram, "From where you are, look carefully in all directions. ¹⁵I am going to give you and your descendants all the land that you see, and it will be yours forever. ¹⁶I am going to give you so many descendants that no one will be able to count them all; it would be as easy to count all the specks of dust on earth! ¹⁷Now, go and look over the whole land, because I am going to give it all to you." ¹⁸So Abram moved his camp and settled near the sacred trees of Mamre at Hebron, and there he built an altar to the LORD.

Abram Rescues Lot

14 Four kings, Amraphel of Babylonia, Arioch of Ellasar, Chedorlaomer of Elam, and Tidal of Goiim, ²went to war against five other kings: Bera of Sodom, Birsha of Gomorrah, Shinab of Admah, Shemeber of Zeboiim, and the king of Bela (or Zoar). ³These five kings had formed an alliance and joined forces in Siddim Valley, which is now the Dead Sea. ⁴They had been under the control of Chedorlaomer for twelve years, but in the thirteenth year they rebelled against him. ⁵In the fourteenth year Chedorlaomer and his allies came with their armies and defeated the Rephaim in Ashteroth Karnaim, the Zuzim in Ham, the Emim in the plain of Kiriathaim, ⁶and the Horites in the mountains of Edom, pursuing them as far as Elparan on the edge of the desert. ⁷Then they turned around and came back to Kadesh (then known as Enmishpat). They conquered all the land of the Amalekites and defeated the Amorites who lived in Hazazon Tamar.

⁸Then the kings of Sodom, Gomorrah, Admah, Zeboiim, and Bela drew up their armies for battle in Siddim Valley and fought ⁹against the kings of Elam, Goiim, Babylonia, and Ellasar, five kings against four. ¹⁰The valley was full of tar pits, and when the kings of Sodom and Gomorrah tried to run away from the battle, they fell into the pits; but the other three

ᵃGARDEN OF THE LORD: *a reference to the Garden of Eden.*
13.10 Gn 2.10   **13.15** Ac 7.5

kings escaped to the mountains. [11]The four kings took everything in Sodom and Gomorrah, including the food, and went away. [12]Lot, Abram's nephew, was living in Sodom, so they took him and all his possessions.

[13]But a man escaped and reported all this to Abram, the Hebrew, who was living near the sacred trees belonging to Mamre the Amorite. Mamre and his brothers Eshcol and Aner were Abram's allies. [14]When Abram heard that his nephew had been captured, he called together all the fighting men in his camp, 318 in all, and pursued the four kings all the way to Dan. [15]There he divided his men into groups, attacked the enemy by night, and defeated them. He chased them as far as Hobah, north of Damascus, [16]and got back all the loot that had been taken. He also brought back his nephew Lot and his possessions, together with the women and the other prisoners.

Melchizedek Blesses Abram

[17]When Abram came back from his victory over Chedorlaomer and the other kings, the king of Sodom went out to meet him in Shaveh Valley (also called King's Valley). [18]And Melchizedek, who was king of Salem and also a priest of the Most High God, brought bread and wine to Abram, [19]blessed him, and said, "May the Most High God, who made heaven and earth, bless Abram! [20]May the Most High God, who gave you victory over your enemies, be praised!" And Abram gave Melchizedek a tenth of all the loot he had recovered.

[21]The king of Sodom said to Abram, "Keep the loot, but give me back all my people."

[22]Abram answered, "I solemnly swear before the LORD, the Most High God, Maker of heaven and earth, [23]that I will not keep anything of yours, not even a thread or a sandal strap. Then you can never say, 'I am the one who made Abram rich.' [24]I will take nothing for myself. I will accept only what my men have used. But let my allies, Aner, Eshcol, and Mamre, take their share."

God's Covenant with Abram

15 After this, Abram had a vision and heard the LORD say to him, "Do not be afraid, Abram. I will shield you from danger and give you a great reward."

[2]But Abram answered, "Sovereign LORD, what good will your reward do me, since I have no children? My only heir is Eliezer of Damascus.[a] [3]You have given me no children, and one of my slaves will inherit my property."

[4]Then he heard the LORD speaking to him again: "This slave Eliezer will not inherit your property; your own son will be your heir." [5]The LORD took him outside and said, "Look at the sky and try to count the stars; you will have as many descendants as that."

[6]Abram put his trust in the LORD, and because of this the LORD was pleased with him and accepted him.

[7]Then the LORD said to him, "I am the LORD, who led you out of Ur in Babylonia, to give you this land as your own."

[8]But Abram asked, "Sovereign LORD, how can I know that it will be mine?"

[9]He answered, "Bring me a cow, a goat, and a ram, each of them three years old, and a dove and a pigeon." [10]Abram brought the animals to God, cut them in half, and placed the halves opposite each other in two rows; but he did not cut up the birds. [11]Vultures came down on the bodies, but Abram drove them off.

[12]When the sun was going down, Abram fell into a deep sleep, and fear and terror came over him. [13]The LORD said to him, "Your descendants will be strangers in a foreign land; they will be slaves there and will be treated cruelly for four hundred years. [14]But I will punish the nation that enslaves them, and when they leave that foreign land, they will take great wealth with them. [15]You yourself will live to a ripe old age, die in peace, and be buried. [16]It will be four generations before your descendants come back here, because I will not drive out the Amorites until they become so wicked that they must be punished."

[17]When the sun had set and it was dark, a smoking fire pot and a flaming torch suddenly appeared and passed between the pieces of the animals. [18]Then and there the LORD made a covenant with Abram. He said, "I promise to give your descendants all this land from the

[a]My . . . Damascus; *Hebrew unclear; literally* The heir of my house, he of Damascus, Eliezer.
14.18-20 He 7.1-10   **15.5** Ro 4.18; He 11.12   **15.6** 1 Macc 2.52; Ro 4.3; Ga 3.6; Jas 2.23   **15.12** Job 4.13, 14   **15.13** Ex 1.1-14; Ac 7.6   **15.14** Ex 12.40, 41; Ac 7.7   **15.18** Ac 7.5

border of Egypt to the Euphrates River, ¹⁹including the lands of the Kenites, the Kenizzites, the Kadmonites, ²⁰the Hittites, the Perizzites, the Rephaim, ²¹the Amorites, the Canaanites, the Girgashites, and the Jebusites."

Hagar and Ishmael

16 Abram's wife Sarai had not borne him any children. But she had an Egyptian slave woman named Hagar, ²and so she said to Abram, "The LORD has kept me from having children. Why don't you sleep with my slave? Perhaps she can have a child for me." Abram agreed with what Sarai said. ³So she gave Hagar to him to be his concubine. (This happened after Abram had lived in Canaan for ten years.) ⁴Abram had intercourse with Hagar, and she became pregnant. When she found out that she was pregnant, she became proud and despised Sarai.

⁵Then Sarai said to Abram, "It's your fault that Hagar despises me.ᵃ I myself gave her to you, and ever since she found out that she was pregnant, she has despised me. May the LORD judge which of us is right, you or me!"

⁶Abram answered, "Very well, she is your slave and under your control; do whatever you want with her." Then Sarai treated Hagar so cruelly that she ran away.

⁷The angel of the LORD met Hagar at a spring in the desert on the road to Shur ⁸and said, "Hagar, slave of Sarai, where have you come from and where are you going?"

She answered, "I am running away from my mistress."

⁹He said, "Go back to her and be her slave." ¹⁰Then he said, "I will give you so many descendants that no one will be able to count them. ¹¹You are going to have a son, and you will name him Ishmael,ᵇ because the LORD has heard your cry of distress. ¹²But your son will live like a wild donkey; he will be against everyone, and everyone will be against him. He will live apart from all his relatives."

¹³Hagar asked herself, "Have I really seen God and lived to tell about it?"ᶜ So she called the LORD, who had spoken to her, "A God Who Sees." ¹⁴That is why people call the well between Kadesh and Bered "The Well of the Living One Who Sees Me."

¹⁵Hagar bore Abram a son, and he named him Ishmael. ¹⁶Abram was eighty-six years old at the time.

Circumcision, the Sign of the Covenant

17 When Abram was ninety-nine years old, the LORD appeared to him and said, "I am the Almighty God. Obey me and always do what is right. ²I will make my covenant with you and give you many descendants." ³Abram bowed down with his face touching the ground, and God said, ⁴"I make this covenant with you: I promise that you will be the ancestor of many nations. ⁵Your name will no longer be Abram, but Abraham,ᵈ because I am making you the ancestor of many nations. ⁶I will give you many descendants, and some of them will be kings. You will have so many descendants that they will become nations.

⁷"I will keep my promise to you and to your descendants in future generations as an everlasting covenant. I will be your God and the God of your descendants. ⁸I will give to you and to your descendants this land in which you are now a foreigner. The whole land of Canaan will belong to your descendants forever, and I will be their God."

⁹God said to Abraham, "You also must agree to keep the covenant with me, both you and your descendants in future generations. ¹⁰You and your descendants must all agree to circumcise every male among you. ¹¹⁻¹²From now on you must circumcise every baby boy when he is eight days old, including slaves born in your homes and slaves bought from foreigners. This will show that there is a covenant between you and me. ¹³Each one must be circumcised, and this will be a physical sign to show that my covenant with you is everlasting. ¹⁴Any male who has not been circumcised will no longer be considered one of my people, because he has not kept the covenant with me."

¹⁵God said to Abraham, "You must no longer call your wife Sarai; from now on her name is Sarah.ᵉ ¹⁶I will bless her, and I will give you a son by her. I will bless her, and she will become the mother of nations, and there will be kings among her descendants."

ᵃIt's your fault . . . me; *or* May you suffer for this wrong done against me.   ᵇISHMAEL: *This name in Hebrew means "God hears."*   ᶜProbable text lived to tell about it?; *Hebrew unclear.*   ᵈABRAHAM: *This name sounds like the Hebrew for "ancestor of many nations."*   ᵉSARAH: *This name in Hebrew means "princess."*

16.15 Ga 4.22   **17.5** Ro 4.17   **17.7** Lk 1.55   **17.8** Ac 7.5   **17.10** Ac 7.8; Ro 4.11

¹⁷Abraham bowed down with his face touching the ground, but he began to laugh when he thought, "Can a man have a child when he is a hundred years old? Can Sarah have a child at ninety?" ¹⁸He asked God, "Why not let Ishmael be my heir?"

¹⁹But God said, "No. Your wife Sarah will bear you a son and you will name him Isaac.ᵃ I will keep my covenant with him and with his descendants forever. It is an everlasting covenant. ²⁰I have heard your request about Ishmael, so I will bless him and give him many children and many descendants. He will be the father of twelve princes, and I will make a great nation of his descendants. ²¹But I will keep my covenant with your son Isaac, who will be born to Sarah about this time next year." ²²When God finished speaking to Abraham, he left him.

²³On that same day Abraham obeyed God and circumcised his son Ishmael and all the other males in his household, including the slaves born in his home and those he had bought. ²⁴Abraham was ninety-nine years old when he was circumcised, ²⁵and his son Ishmael was thirteen. ²⁶They were both circumcised on the same day, ²⁷together with all of Abraham's slaves.

A Son Is Promised to Abraham

18 The LORD appeared to Abraham at the sacred trees of Mamre. As Abraham was sitting at the entrance of his tent during the hottest part of the day, ²he looked up and saw three men standing there. As soon as he saw them, he ran out to meet them. Bowing down with his face touching the ground, ³he said, "Sirs, please do not pass by my home without stopping; I am here to serve you. ⁴Let me bring some water for you to wash your feet; you can rest here beneath this tree. ⁵I will also bring a bit of food; it will give you strength to continue your journey. You have honored me by coming to my home, so let me serve you."

They replied, "Thank you; we accept."

⁶Abraham hurried into the tent and said to Sarah, "Quick, take a sack of your best flour, and bake some bread." ⁷Then he ran to the herd and picked out a calf that was tender and fat, and gave it to a servant, who hurried to get it ready. ⁸He took some cream, some milk, and the meat, and set the food before the men. There under the tree he served them himself, and they ate.

⁹Then they asked him, "Where is your wife Sarah?"

"She is there in the tent," he answered.

¹⁰One of them said, "Nine months from nowᵇ I will come back, and your wife Sarah will have a son."

Sarah was behind him, at the door of the tent, listening. ¹¹Abraham and Sarah were very old, and Sarah had stopped having her monthly periods. ¹²So Sarah laughed to herself and said, "Now that I am old and worn out, can I still enjoy sex? And besides, my husband is old too."

¹³Then the LORD asked Abraham, "Why did Sarah laugh and say, 'Can I really have a child when I am so old?' ¹⁴Is anything too hard for the LORD? As I said, nine months from now I will return, and Sarah will have a son."

¹⁵Because Sarah was afraid, she denied it. "I didn't laugh," she said.

"Yes, you did," he replied. "You laughed."

Abraham Pleads for Sodom

¹⁶Then the men left and went to a place where they could look down at Sodom, and Abraham went with them to send them on their way. ¹⁷And the LORD said to himself, "I will not hide from Abraham what I am going to do. ¹⁸His descendants will become a great and mighty nation, and through him I will bless all the nations.ᶜ ¹⁹I have chosen him in order that he may command his sons and his descendants to obey me and to do what is right and just. If they do, I will do everything for him that I have promised."

²⁰Then the LORD said to Abraham, "There are terrible accusations against Sodom and Gomorrah, and their sin is very great. ²¹I must go down to find out whether or not the accusations which I have heard are true."

²²Then the two men left and went on toward Sodom, but the LORD remained with Abraham. ²³Abraham approached the LORD and asked, "Are you really going to destroy the in-

---

ᵃISAAC: *This name in Hebrew means "he laughs."*   ᵇNine months from now; *or* This time next year.
ᶜthrough . . . nations; *or* all the nations will ask me to bless them as I have blessed him.
18.2 a He 13.2   **18.10** Ro 9.9   **18.12** 1 P 3.6   **18.14** Lk 1.37

nocent with the guilty? 24If there are fifty innocent people in the city, will you destroy the whole city? Won't you spare it in order to save the fifty? 25Surely you won't kill the innocent with the guilty. That's impossible! You can't do that. If you did, the innocent would be punished along with the guilty. That is impossible. The judge of all the earth has to act justly."

26The LORD answered, "If I find fifty innocent people in Sodom, I will spare the whole city for their sake."

27Abraham spoke again: "Please forgive my boldness in continuing to speak to you, Lord. I am only a man and have no right to say anything. 28But perhaps there will be only forty-five innocent people instead of fifty. Will you destroy the whole city because there are five too few?"

The LORD answered, "I will not destroy the city if I find forty-five innocent people."

29Abraham spoke again: "Perhaps there will be only forty."

He replied, "I will not destroy it if there are forty."

30Abraham said, "Please don't be angry, Lord, but I must speak again. What if there are only thirty?"

He said, "I will not do it if I find thirty."

31Abraham said, "Please forgive my boldness in continuing to speak to you, Lord. Suppose that only twenty are found?"

He said, "I will not destroy the city if I find twenty."

32Abraham said, "Please don't be angry, Lord, and I will speak only once more. What if only ten are found?"

He said, "I will not destroy it if there are ten." 33After he had finished speaking with Abraham, the LORD went away, and Abraham returned home.

The Sinfulness of Sodom

19 When the two angels came to Sodom that evening, Lot was sitting at the city gate. As soon as he saw them, he got up and went to meet them. He bowed down before them 2and said, "Sirs, I am here to serve you. Please come to my house. You can wash your feet and spend the night. In the morning you can get up early and go on your way."

But they answered, "No, we will spend the night here in the city square."

3He kept on urging them, and finally they went with him to his house. Lot ordered his servants to bake some bread and prepare a fine meal for the guests. When it was ready, they ate it.

4Before the guests went to bed, the men of Sodom surrounded the house. All the men of the city, both young and old, were there. 5They called out to Lot and asked, "Where are the men who came to stay with you tonight? Bring them out to us!" The men of Sodom wanted to have sex with them.

6Lot went outside and closed the door behind him. 7He said to them, "Friends, I beg you, don't do such a wicked thing! 8Look, I have two daughters who are still virgins. Let me bring them out to you, and you can do whatever you want with them. But don't do anything to these men; they are guests in my house, and I must protect them."

9But they said, "Get out of our way, you foreigner! Who are you to tell us what to do? Out of our way, or we will treat you worse than them." They pushed Lot back and moved up to break down the door. 10But the two men inside reached out, pulled Lot back into the house, and shut the door. 11Then they struck all the men outside with blindness, so that they couldn't find the door.

Lot Leaves Sodom

12The two men said to Lot, "If you have anyone else here—sons, daughters, sons-in-law, or any other relatives living in the city—get them out of here, 13because we are going to destroy this place. The LORD has heard the terrible accusations against these people and has sent us to destroy Sodom."

14Then Lot went to the men that his daughters were going to marry, and said, "Hurry up and get out of here; the LORD is going to destroy this place." But they thought he was joking.

15At dawn the angels tried to make Lot hurry. "Quick!" they said. "Take your wife and your two daughters and get out, so that you will not lose your lives when the city is destroyed."

19.5-8 Jg 19.22-24   **19.11** 2 K 6.18

¹⁶Lot hesitated. The LORD, however, had pity on him; so the men took him, his wife, and his two daughters by the hand and led them out of the city. ¹⁷Then one of the angels said, "Run for your lives! Don't look back and don't stop in the valley. Run to the hills, so that you won't be killed."

¹⁸But Lot answered, "No, please don't make us do that, sir. ¹⁹You have done me a great favor and saved my life. But the hills are too far away; the disaster will overtake me, and I will die before I get there. ²⁰Do you see that little town? It is near enough. Let me go over there—you can see it is just a small place—and I will be safe."

²¹He answered, "All right, I agree. I won't destroy that town. ²²Hurry! Run! I can't do anything until you get there."

Because Lot called it small, the town was named Zoar.ᵃ

The Destruction of Sodom and Gomorrah

²³The sun was rising when Lot reached Zoar. ²⁴Suddenly the LORD rained burning sulfur on the cities of Sodom and Gomorrah ²⁵and destroyed them and the whole valley, along with all the people there and everything that grew on the land. ²⁶But Lot's wife looked back and was turned into a pillar of salt.

²⁷Early the next morning Abraham hurried to the place where he had stood in the presence of the LORD. ²⁸He looked down at Sodom and Gomorrah and the whole valley and saw smoke rising from the land, like smoke from a huge furnace. ²⁹But when God destroyed the cities of the valley where Lot was living, he kept Abraham in mind and allowed Lot to escape to safety.

Lot's wife looked back. (19.26)

The Origin of the Moabites and Ammonites

³⁰Because Lot was afraid to stay in Zoar, he and his two daughters moved up into the hills and lived in a cave. ³¹The older daughter said to her sister, "Our father is getting old, and there are no men in the whole worldᵇ to marry us so that we can have children. ³²Come on, let's get our father drunk, so that we can sleep with him and have children by him." ³³That night they gave him wine to drink, and the older daughter had intercourse with him. But he was so drunk that he didn't know it.

³⁴The next day the older daughter said to her sister, "I slept with him last night; now let's get him drunk again tonight, and you sleep with him. Then each of us will have a child by our father." ³⁵So that night they got him drunk, and the younger daughter had intercourse with him. Again he was so drunk that he didn't know it. ³⁶In this way both of Lot's daughters became pregnant by their own father. ³⁷The older daughter had a son, whom she named Moab.ᶜ He was the ancestor of the present-day Moabites. ³⁸The younger daughter also had a son, whom she named Benammi.ᵈ He was the ancestor of the present-day Ammonites.

Abraham and Abimelech

20 Abraham moved from Mamre to the southern part of Canaan and lived between Kadesh and Shur. Later, while he was living in Gerar, ²he said that his wife Sarah was his sister. So King Abimelech of Gerar had Sarah brought to him. ³One night God appeared to him in a dream and said, "You are going to die, because you have taken this woman; she is already married."

ᵃZOAR: *This name sounds like the Hebrew for "small."*   ᵇthe whole world; *or* this land.   ᶜMOAB: *This name sounds like the Hebrew for "from my father."*   ᵈBENAMMI: *This name in Hebrew means "son of my relative" and sounds like the Hebrew for "Ammonite."*

19.16 2 P 2.7   **19.24, 25** Mt 10.15; 11.23, 24; Lk 10.12; 17.29; 2 P 2.6; Jd 7   **19.26** Ws 10.7; Lk 17.32
20.2 Gn 12.13; 26.7

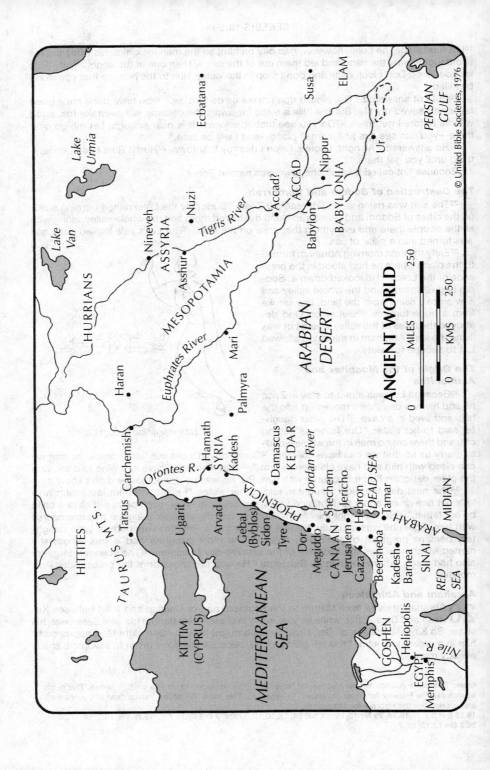

ANCIENT WORLD

© United Bible Societies, 1976

MILES 250
KMS 250
0

PERSIAN GULF

ELAM

Susa
Ecbatana

ACCAD
Babylon
Nippur
BABYLONIA
Ur
Accad?

Lake Urmia

Lake Van

Nuzi
Nineveh
ASSYRIA
Asshur
Tigris River

HURRIANS

MESOPOTAMIA

Euphrates River

Mari
Palmyra

ARABIAN DESERT

Haran

KEDAR

Carchemish
Hamath
Orontes R.
Kadesh
SYRIA
Damascus
Jordan River

TAURUS MTS.

Tarsus

HITTITES

Ugarit
Arvad
Gebal (Byblos)
Sidon
Tyre
Dor
Megiddo
Shechem
Jericho
Jerusalem
Hebron
CANAAN
Gaza
Beersheba
PHOENICIA
DEAD SEA
Tamar
ARABAH
MIDIAN

KITTIM (CYPRUS)

MEDITERRANEAN SEA

Kadesh Barnea
SINAI
RED SEA

GOSHEN
Heliopolis
EGYPT
Memphis
Nile R.

⁴But Abimelech had not come near her, and he said, "Lord, I am innocent! Would you destroy me and my people? ⁵Abraham himself said that she was his sister, and she said the same thing. I did this with a clear conscience, and I have done no wrong."

⁶God replied in the dream, "Yes, I know that you did it with a clear conscience; so I kept you from sinning against me and did not let you touch her. ⁷But now, give the woman back to her husband. He is a prophet, and he will pray for you, so that you will not die. But if you do not give her back, I warn you that you are going to die, you and all your people."

⁸Early the next morning Abimelech called all his officials and told them what had happened, and they were terrified. ⁹Then Abimelech called Abraham and asked, "What have you done to us? What wrong have I done to you to make you bring this disaster on me and my kingdom? No one should ever do what you have done to me. ¹⁰Why did you do it?"

¹¹Abraham answered, "I thought that there would be no one here who has reverence for God and that they would kill me to get my wife. ¹²She really is my sister. She is the daughter of my father, but not of my mother, and I married her. ¹³So when God sent me from my father's house into foreign lands, I said to her, 'You can show how loyal you are to me by telling everyone that I am your brother.' "

¹⁴Then Abimelech gave Sarah back to Abraham, and at the same time he gave him sheep, cattle, and slaves. ¹⁵He said to Abraham, "Here is my whole land; live anywhere you like." ¹⁶He said to Sarah, "I am giving your brother a thousand pieces of silver as proof to all who are with you that you are innocent; everyone will know that you have done no wrong."

¹⁷⁻¹⁸Because of what had happened to Sarah, Abraham's wife, the LORD had made it impossible for any woman in Abimelech's palace to have children. So Abraham prayed for Abimelech, and God healed him. He also healed his wife and his slave women, so that they could have children.

The Birth of Isaac

21 The LORD blessed Sarah, as he had promised, ²and she became pregnant and bore a son to Abraham when he was old. The boy was born at the time God had said he would be born. ³Abraham named him Isaac, ⁴and when Isaac was eight days old, Abraham circumcised him, as God had commanded. ⁵Abraham was a hundred years old when Isaac was born. ⁶Sarah said, "God has brought me joy and laughter.ᵃ Everyone who hears about it will laugh with me." ⁷Then she added, "Who would have said to Abraham that Sarah would nurse children? Yet I have borne him a son in his old age."

⁸The child grew, and on the day that he was weaned, Abraham gave a great feast.

Hagar and Ishmael Are Sent Away

⁹One day Ishmael, whom Hagar the Egyptian had borne to Abraham, was playing withᵇ Sarah's son Isaac.ᶜ ¹⁰Sarah saw them and said to Abraham, "Send this slave and her son away. The son of this woman must not get any part of your wealth, which my son Isaac should inherit." ¹¹This troubled Abraham very much, because Ishmael also was his son. ¹²But God said to Abraham, "Don't be worried about the boy and your slave Hagar. Do whatever Sarah tells you, because it is through Isaac that you will have the descendants I have promised. ¹³I will also give many children to the son of the slave woman, so that they will become a nation. He too is your son."

¹⁴Early the next morning Abraham gave Hagar some food and a leather bag full of water. He put the child on her back and sent her away. She left and wandered about in the wilderness of Beersheba. ¹⁵When the water was all gone, she left the child under a bush ¹⁶and sat down about a hundred yards away. She said to herself, "I can't bear to see my child die." While she was sitting there, sheᵈ began to cry.

¹⁷God heard the boy crying, and from heaven the angel of God spoke to Hagar, "What are you troubled about, Hagar? Don't be afraid. God has heard the boy crying. ¹⁸Get up, go and pick him up, and comfort him. I will make a great nation out of his descendants." ¹⁹Then God opened her eyes, and she saw a well. She went and filled the leather bag with water

---

ᵃLAUGHTER: *The name Isaac in Hebrew means "he laughs" (see also 17.17-19).*   ᵇplaying with; *or* making fun of.   ᶜ*Some ancient translations* with Sarah's son Isaac; *Hebrew does not have these words.*   ᵈshe; *one ancient translation* the child.
21.2 He 11.11   **21.4** Gn 17.12; Ac 7.8   **21.10** Ga 4.29, 30   **21.12** Ro 9.7; He 11.18

and gave some to the boy. 20God was with the boy as he grew up; he lived in the wilderness of Paran and became a skillful hunter. 21His mother got an Egyptian wife for him.

The Agreement between Abraham and Abimelech

22At that time Abimelech went with Phicol, the commander of his army, and said to Abraham, "God is with you in everything you do. 23So make a vow here in the presence of God that you will not deceive me, my children, or my descendants. I have been loyal to you, so promise that you will also be loyal to me and to this country in which you are living."

24Abraham said, "I promise."

25Abraham complained to Abimelech about a well which the servants of Abimelech had seized. 26Abimelech said, "I don't know who did this. You didn't tell me about it, and this is the first I have heard of it." 27Then Abraham gave some sheep and cattle to Abimelech, and the two of them made an agreement. 28Abraham separated seven lambs from his flock, 29and Abimelech asked him, "Why did you do that?"

30Abraham answered, "Accept these seven lambs. By doing this, you admit that I am the one who dug this well." 31And so the place was called Beersheba,a because it was there that the two of them made a vow.

32After they had made this agreement at Beersheba, Abimelech and Phicol went back to Philistia. 33Then Abraham planted a tamarisk tree in Beersheba and worshiped the LORD, the Everlasting God. 34Abraham lived in Philistia for a long time.

God Commands Abraham to Offer Isaac

22 Some time later God tested Abraham; he called to him, "Abraham!" And Abraham answered, "Yes, here I am!"

2"Take your son," God said, "your only son, Isaac, whom you love so much, and go to the land of Moriah. There on a mountain that I will show you, offer him as a sacrifice to me."

3Early the next morning Abraham cut some wood for the sacrifice, loaded his donkey, and took Isaac and two servants with him. They started out for the place that God had told him about. 4On the third day Abraham saw the place in the distance. 5Then he said to the servants, "Stay here with the donkey. The boy and I will go over there and worship, and then we will come back to you."

6Abraham made Isaac carry the wood for the sacrifice, and he himself carried a knife and live coals for starting the fire. As they walked along together, 7Isaac spoke up, "Father!"

He answered, "Yes, my son?"

Isaac asked, "I see that you have the coals and the wood, but where is the lamb for the sacrifice?"

8Abraham answered, "God himself will provide one." And the two of them walked on together.

9When they came to the place which God had told him about, Abraham built an altar and arranged the wood on it. He tied up his son and placed him on the altar, on top of the wood. 10Then he picked up the knife to kill him. 11But the angel of the LORD called to him from heaven, "Abraham, Abraham!"

He answered, "Yes, here I am."

12"Don't hurt the boy or do anything to him," he said. "Now I know that you honor and obey God, because you have not kept back your only son from him."

13Abraham looked around and saw a ram caught in a bush by its horns. He went and got it and offered it as a burnt offering instead of his son. 14Abraham named that place "The LORD Provides."b And even today people say, "On the LORD's mountain he provides."c

15The angel of the LORD called to Abraham from heaven a second time, 16"I make a vow by my own name—the LORD is speaking—that I will richly bless you. Because you did this and did not keep back your only son from me, 17I promise that I will give you as many descendants as there are stars in the sky or grains of sand along the seashore. Your descend-

---

aBEERSHEBA: This name in Hebrew means "Well of the Vow" or "Well of Seven" (see also 26.33).　　bProvides; or Sees.　　cprovides; or is seen.

21.22 Gn 26.26　　**22.1-13** Ws 10.5; Si 44.20; He 11.17-19　　**22.2** 2 Ch 3.1　　**22.9** Jas 2.21　　**22.16, 17** He 6.13, 14　　**22.17** He 11.12

ants will conquer their enemies. [18]All the nations will ask me to bless them as I have blessed your descendants—all because you obeyed my command." [19]Abraham went back to his servants, and they went together to Beersheba, where Abraham settled.

The Descendants of Nahor
[20]Some time later Abraham learned that Milcah had borne eight children to his brother Nahor: [21]Uz the first-born, Buz his brother, Kemuel the father of Aram, [22]Chesed, Hazo, Pildash, Jidlaph, and Bethuel, [23]Rebecca's father. Milcah bore these eight sons to Nahor, Abraham's brother. [24]Reumah, Nahor's concubine, bore Tebah, Gaham, Tahash, and Maacah.

"Now I know that you honor and obey God." (22.12)

Sarah Dies and Abraham Buys a Burial Ground
23 Sarah lived to be 127 years old. [2]She died in Hebron in the land of Canaan, and Abraham mourned her death.

[3]He left the place where his wife's body was lying, went to the Hittites, and said, [4]"I am a foreigner living here among you; sell me some land, so that I can bury my wife."

[5]They answered, [6]"Listen to us, sir. We look upon you as a mighty leader; bury your wife in the best grave that we have. Any of us would be glad to give you a grave, so that you can bury her."

[7]Then Abraham bowed before them [8]and said, "If you are willing to let me bury my wife here, please ask Ephron son of Zohar [9]to sell me Machpelah Cave, which is near the edge of his field. Ask him to sell it to me for its full price, here in your presence, so that I can own it as a burial ground."

[10]Ephron himself was sitting with the other Hittites at the meeting place at the city gate; he answered in the hearing of everyone there, [11]"Listen, sir; I will give you the whole field and the cave that is in it. Here in the presence of my own people, I will give it to you, so that you can bury your wife."

[12]But Abraham bowed before the Hittites [13]and said to Ephron, so that everyone could hear, "May I ask you, please, to listen. I will buy the whole field. Accept my payment, and I will bury my wife there."

[14]Ephron answered, [15]"Sir, land worth only four hundred pieces of silver—what is that between us? Bury your wife in it." [16]Abraham agreed and weighed out the amount that Ephron had mentioned in the hearing of the people—four hundred pieces of silver, according to the standard weights used by the merchants.

[17]That is how the property which had belonged to Ephron at Machpelah east of Mamre, became Abraham's. It included the field, the cave which was in it, and all the trees in the field up to the edge of the property. [18]It was recognized as Abraham's property by all the Hittites who were there at the meeting.

[19]Then Abraham buried his wife Sarah in that cave in the land of Canaan. [20]So the field which had belonged to the Hittites, and the cave in it, became the property of Abraham for a burial ground.

A Wife for Isaac
24 Abraham was now very old, and the LORD had blessed him in everything he did. [2]He said to his oldest servant, who was in charge of all that he had, "Place your hand between my thighs[a] and make a vow. [3]I want you to make a vow in the name of the LORD, the

---

[a]PLACE . . . THIGHS: *This was the way in which a vow was made absolutely unchangeable.*
22.18 Ac 3.25   **23.4** He 11.9, 13; Ac 7.16

God of heaven and earth, that you will not choose a wife for my son from the people here in Canaan. ⁴You must go back to the country where I was born and get a wife for my son Isaac from among my relatives."

⁵But the servant asked, "What if the young woman will not leave home to come with me to this land? Shall I send your son back to the land you came from?"

⁶Abraham answered, "Make sure that you don't send my son back there! ⁷The LORD, the God of heaven, brought me from the home of my father and from the land of my relatives, and he solemnly promised me that he would give this land to my descendants. He will send his angel before you, so that you can get a wife there for my son. ⁸If the young woman is not willing to come with you, you will be free from this promise. But you must not under any circumstances take my son back there." ⁹So the servant put his hand between the thighs of Abraham, his master, and made a vow to do what Abraham had asked.

¹⁰The servant, who was in charge of Abraham's property, took ten of his master's camels and went to the city where Nahor had lived in northern Mesopotamia. ¹¹When he arrived, he made the camels kneel down at the well outside the city. It was late afternoon, the time when women came out to get water. ¹²He prayed, "LORD, God of my master Abraham, give me success today and keep your promise to my master. ¹³Here I am at the well where the young women of the city will be coming to get water. ¹⁴I will say to one of them, 'Please, lower your jar and let me have a drink.' If she says, 'Drink, and I will also bring water for your camels,' may she be the one that you have chosen for your servant Isaac. If this happens, I will know that you have kept your promise to my master."

¹⁵Before he had finished praying, Rebecca arrived with a water jar on her shoulder. She was the daughter of Bethuel, who was the son of Abraham's brother Nahor and his wife Milcah. ¹⁶She was a very beautiful young woman and still a virgin. She went down to the well, filled her jar, and came back. ¹⁷The servant ran to meet her and said, "Please give me a drink of water from your jar."

¹⁸She said, "Drink, sir," and quickly lowered her jar from her shoulder and held it while he drank. ¹⁹When he had finished, she said, "I will also bring water for your camels and let them have all they want." ²⁰She

Rebecca arrived. (24.15)

quickly emptied her jar into the animals' drinking trough and ran to the well to get more water, until she had watered all his camels. ²¹The man kept watching her in silence, to see if the LORD had given him success.

²²When she had finished, the man took an expensive gold ring and put it in her nose and put two large gold bracelets on her arms. ²³He said, "Please tell me who your father is. Is there room in his house for my men and me to spend the night?"

²⁴"My father is Bethuel son of Nahor and Milcah," she answered. ²⁵"There is plenty of straw and fodder at our house, and there is a place for you to stay."

²⁶Then the man knelt down and worshiped the LORD. ²⁷He said, "Praise the LORD, the God of my master Abraham, who has faithfully kept his promise to my master. The LORD has led me straight to my master's relatives."

²⁸The young woman ran to her mother's house and told the whole story. ²⁹Now Rebecca had a brother named Laban, and he ran outside to go to the well where Abraham's servant was. ³⁰Laban had seen the nose ring and the bracelets on his sister's arms and had heard her say what the man had told her. He went to Abraham's servant, who was standing by his camels at the well, ³¹and said, "Come home with me. You are a man whom the LORD has blessed. Why are you standing out here? I have a room ready for you in my house, and there is a place for your camels."

³²So the man went into the house, and Laban unloaded the camels and gave them straw and fodder. Then he brought water for Abraham's servant and his men to wash their

feet. 33When food was brought, the man said, "I will not eat until I have said what I have to say."

Laban said, "Go on and speak."

34"I am the servant of Abraham," he began. 35"The LORD has greatly blessed my master and made him a rich man. He has given him flocks of sheep and goats, cattle, silver, gold, male and female slaves, camels, and donkeys. 36Sarah, my master's wife, bore him a son when she was old, and my master has given everything he owns to him. 37My master made me promise with a vow to obey his command. He said, 'Do not choose a wife for my son from the young women in the land of Canaan. 38Instead, go to my father's people, to my relatives, and choose a wife for him.' 39And I asked my master, 'What if she will not come with me?' 40He answered, 'The LORD, whom I have always obeyed, will send his angel with you and give you success. You will get for my son a wife from my own people, from my father's family. 41There is only one way for you to be free from your vow: if you go to my relatives and they refuse you, then you will be free.'

42"When I came to the well today, I prayed, 'LORD, God of my master Abraham, please give me success in what I am doing. 43Here I am at the well. When a young woman comes out to get water, I will ask her to give me a drink of water from her jar. 44If she agrees and also offers to bring water for my camels, may she be the one that you have chosen as the wife for my master's son.' 45Before I had finished my silent prayer, Rebecca came with a water jar on her shoulder and went down to the well to get water. I said to her, 'Please give me a drink.' 46She quickly lowered her jar from her shoulder and said, 'Drink, and I will also water your camels.' So I drank, and she watered the camels. 47I asked her, 'Who is your father?' And she answered, 'My father is Bethuel son of Nahor and Milcah.' Then I put the ring in her nose and the bracelets on her arms. 48I knelt down and worshiped the LORD. I praised the LORD, the God of my master Abraham, who had led me straight to my master's relative, where I found his daughter for my master's son. 49Now, if you intend to fulfill your responsibility toward my master and treat him fairly, please tell me; if not, say so, and I will decide what to do."

50Laban and Bethuel answered, "Since this matter comes from the LORD, it is not for us to make a decision. 51Here is Rebecca; take her and go. Let her become the wife of your master's son, as the LORD himself has said." 52When the servant of Abraham heard this, he bowed down and worshiped the LORD. 53Then he brought out clothing and silver and gold jewelry, and gave them to Rebecca. He also gave expensive gifts to her brother and to her mother.

54Then Abraham's servant and the men with him ate and drank, and spent the night there. When they got up in the morning, he said, "Let me go back to my master."

55But Rebecca's brother and her mother said, "Let her stay with us a week or ten days, and then she may go."

56But he said, "Don't make us stay. The LORD has made my journey a success; let me go back to my master."

57They answered, "Let's call her and find out what she has to say." 58So they called Rebecca and asked, "Do you want to go with this man?"

"Yes," she answered.

59So they let Rebecca and her old family servant go with Abraham's servant and his men. 60And they gave Rebecca their blessing in these words:

"May you, sister, become the mother of millions!
May your descendants conquer the cities of their enemies!"

61Then Rebecca and her young women got ready and mounted the camels to go with Abraham's servant, and they all started out.

62Isaac had come into the wilderness ofa "The Well of the Living One Who Sees Me" and was staying in the southern part of Canaan. 63He went out in the early evening to take a walk in the fields and saw camels coming. 64When Rebecca saw Isaac, she got down from her camel 65and asked Abraham's servant, "Who is that man walking toward us in the field?"

"He is my master," the servant answered. So she took her scarf and covered her face.

66The servant told Isaac everything he had done. 67Then Isaac brought Rebecca into the tent that his mother Sarah had lived in, and she became his wife. Isaac loved Rebecca, and so he was comforted for the loss of his mother.

aSome ancient translations into the wilderness of; Hebrew from coming.

Other Descendants of Abraham
(1 Chronicles 1.32, 33)

25 Abraham married another woman, whose name was Keturah. [2]She bore him Zimran, Jokshan, Medan, Midian, Ishbak, and Shuah. [3]Jokshan was the father of Sheba and Dedan, and the descendants of Dedan were the Asshurim, the Letushim, and the Leummim. [4]The sons of Midian were Ephah, Epher, Hanoch, Abida, and Eldaah. All these were Keturah's descendants.

[5]Abraham left everything he owned to Isaac; [6]but while he was still alive, he gave presents to the sons his other wives had borne him. Then he sent these sons to the land of the East, away from his son Isaac.

The Death and Burial of Abraham

[7-8]Abraham died at the ripe old age of 175. [9]His sons Isaac and Ishmael buried him in Machpelah Cave, in the field east of Mamre that had belonged to Ephron son of Zohar the Hittite. [10]It was the field that Abraham had bought from the Hittites; both Abraham and his wife Sarah were buried there. [11]After the death of Abraham, God blessed his son Isaac, who lived near "The Well of the Living One Who Sees Me."

The Descendants of Ishmael
(1 Chronicles 1.28-31)

[12]Ishmael, whom Hagar, the Egyptian slave of Sarah, bore to Abraham, [13]had the following sons, listed in the order of their birth: Nebaioth, Kedar, Adbeel, Mibsam, [14]Mishma, Dumah, Massa, [15]Hadad, Tema, Jetur, Naphish, and Kedemah. [16]They were the ancestors of twelve tribes, and their names were given to their villages and camping places. [17]Ishmael was 137 years old when he died. [18]The descendants of Ishmael lived in the territory between Havilah and Shur, to the east of Egypt on the way to Assyria. They lived apart from the other descendants of Abraham.

The Birth of Esau and Jacob

[19]This is the story of Abraham's son Isaac. [20]Isaac was forty years old when he married Rebecca, the daughter of Bethuel (an Aramean from Mesopotamia) and sister of Laban. [21]Because Rebecca had no children, Isaac prayed to the LORD for her. The LORD answered his prayer, and Rebecca became pregnant. [22]She was going to have twins, and before they were born, they struggled against each other in her womb. She said, "Why should something like this happen to me?" So she went to ask the LORD for an answer.

[23]The LORD said to her,

"Two nations are within you;
You will give birth to two rival peoples.
One will be stronger than the other;
The older will serve the younger."

[24]The time came for her to give birth, and she had twin sons. [25]The first one was reddish, and his skin was like a hairy robe, so he was named Esau.[a] [26]The second one was born holding on tightly to the heel of Esau, so he was named Jacob.[b] Isaac was sixty years old when they were born.

Esau Sells His Rights as the First-Born Son

[27]The boys grew up, and Esau became a skilled hunter, a man who loved the outdoors, but Jacob was a quiet man who stayed at home. [28]Isaac preferred Esau, because he enjoyed eating the animals Esau killed, but Rebecca preferred Jacob.

[29]One day while Jacob was cooking some bean soup, Esau came in from hunting. He was hungry [30]and said to Jacob, "I'm starving; give me some of that red stuff." (That is why he was named Edom.[c])

[31]Jacob answered, "I will give it to you if you give me your rights as the first-born son."

---

[a]ESAU: *This name is taken to refer to Seir, the territory later inhabited by Esau's descendants; Seir sounds like the Hebrew for "hairy."*   [b]JACOB: *This name sounds like the Hebrew for "heel."*   [c]EDOM: *This name sounds like the Hebrew for "red."*
25.10 Gn 23.3-16   **25.23** Ro 9.12

32Esau said, "All right! I am about to die; what good will my rights do me?"

33Jacob answered, "First make a vow that you will give me your rights."

Esau made the vow and gave his rights to Jacob. **34**Then Jacob gave him some bread and some of the soup. He ate and drank and then got up and left. That was all Esau cared about his rights as the first-born son.

Isaac Lives at Gerar

26 There was another famine in the land besides the earlier one during the time of Abraham. Isaac went to Abimelech, king of the Philistines, at Gerar. **2**The LORD had appeared to Isaac and had said, "Do not go to Egypt; stay in this land, where I tell you to stay. **3**Live here, and I will be with you and bless you. I am going to give all this territory to you and to your descendants. I will keep the promise I made to your father Abraham. **4**I will give you as many descendants as there

Then Jacob gave him . . . some of the soup. (25.34)

are stars in the sky, and I will give them all this territory. All the nations will ask me to bless them as I have blessed your descendants. **5**I will bless you, because Abraham obeyed me and kept all my laws and commands."

6So Isaac lived at Gerar. **7**When the men there asked about his wife, he said that she was his sister. He would not admit that she was his wife, because he was afraid that the men there would kill him to get Rebecca, who was very beautiful. **8**When Isaac had been there for some time, King Abimelech looked down from his window and saw Isaac and Rebecca making love. **9**Abimelech sent for Isaac and said, "So she is your wife! Why did you say she was your sister?"

He answered, "I thought I would be killed if I said she was my wife."

10"What have you done to us?" Abimelech said. "One of my men might easily have slept with your wife, and you would have been responsible for our guilt." **11**Abimelech warned all the people: "Anyone who mistreats this man or his wife will be put to death."

12Isaac sowed crops in that land, and that year he harvested a hundred times as much as he had sown, because the LORD blessed him. **13**He continued to prosper and became a very rich man. **14**Because he had many herds of sheep and cattle and many servants, the Philistines were jealous of him. **15**So they filled in all the wells which the servants of his father Abraham had dug while Abraham was alive.

16Then Abimelech said to Isaac, "Leave our country. You have become more powerful than we are." **17**So Isaac left and set up his camp in Gerar Valley, where he stayed for some time. **18**He dug once again the wells which had been dug during the time of Abraham and which the Philistines had stopped up after Abraham's death. Isaac gave the wells the same names that his father had given them.

19Isaac's servants dug a well in the valley and found water. **20**The shepherds of Gerar quarreled with Isaac's shepherds and said, "This water belongs to us." So Isaac named the well "Quarrel."

21Isaac's servants dug another well, and there was a quarrel about that one also, so he named it "Enmity." **22**He moved away from there and dug another well. There was no dispute about this one, so he named it "Freedom." He said, "Now the LORD has given us freedom to live in the land, and we will be prosperous here."

23Isaac left and went to Beersheba. **24**That night the LORD appeared to him and said, "I am the God of your father Abraham. Do not be afraid; I am with you. I will bless you and give

25.33 He 12.16   **26.3, 4** Gn 22.16-18   **26.7** Gn 12.13; 20.2

you many descendants because of my promise to my servant Abraham." [25]Isaac built an altar there and worshiped the LORD. Then he set up his camp there, and his servants dug another well.

The Agreement between Isaac and Abimelech

[26]Abimelech came from Gerar with Ahuzzath his adviser and Phicol the commander of his army to see Isaac. [27]So Isaac asked, "Why have you now come to see me, when you were so unfriendly to me before and made me leave your country?"

[28]They answered, "Now we know that the LORD is with you, and we think that there should be a solemn agreement between us. We want you to promise [29]that you will not harm us, just as we did not harm you. We were kind to you and let you go peacefully. Now it is clear that the LORD has blessed you." [30]Isaac prepared a feast for them, and they ate and drank. [31]Early next morning each man made his promise and sealed it with a vow. Isaac said goodbye to them, and they parted as friends.

[32]On that day Isaac's servants came and told him about the well which they had dug. They said, "We have found water." [33]He named the well "Vow." That is how the city of Beersheba[a] got its name.

Esau's Foreign Wives

[34]When Esau was forty years old, he married two Hittites, Judith the daughter of Beeri, and Basemath the daughter of Elon. [35]They made life miserable for Isaac and Rebecca.

Isaac Blesses Jacob

27 Isaac was now old and had become blind. He sent for his older son Esau and said to him, "Son!"

"Yes," he answered.

[2]Isaac said, "You see that I am old and may die soon. [3]Take your bow and arrows, go out into the country, and kill an animal for me. [4]Cook me some of that tasty food that I like, and bring it to me. After I have eaten it, I will give you my final blessing before I die."

[5]While Isaac was talking to Esau, Rebecca was listening. So when Esau went out to hunt, [6]she said to Jacob, "I have just heard your father say to Esau, [7]'Bring me an animal and cook it for me. After I have eaten it, I will give you my blessing in the presence of the LORD before I die.' [8]Now, son," Rebecca continued, "listen to me and do what I say. [9]Go to the flock and pick out two fat young goats, so that I can cook them and make some of that food your father likes so much. [10]You can take it to him to eat, and he will give you his blessing before he dies."

[11]But Jacob said to his mother, "You know that Esau is a hairy man, but I have smooth skin. [12]Perhaps my father will touch me and find out that I am deceiving him; in this way, I will bring a curse on myself instead of a blessing."

[13]His mother answered, "Let any curse against you fall on me, my son; just do as I say, and go and get the goats for me." [14]So he went to get them and brought them to her, and she cooked the kind of food that his father liked. [15]Then she took Esau's best clothes, which she kept in the house, and put them on Jacob. [16]She put the skins of the goats on his arms and on the hairless part of his neck. [17]She handed him the tasty food, along with the bread she had baked.

[18]Then Jacob went to his father and said, "Father!"

"Yes," he answered. "Which of my sons are you?"

[19]Jacob answered, "I am your older son Esau; I have done as you told me. Please sit up and eat some of the meat that I have brought you, so that you can give me your blessing."

[20]Isaac said, "How did you find it so quickly, son?"

Jacob answered, "The LORD your God helped me find it."

[21]Isaac said to Jacob, "Please come closer so that I can touch you. Are you really Esau?" [22]Jacob moved closer to his father, who felt him and said, "Your voice sounds like Jacob's voice, but your arms feel like Esau's arms." [23]He did not recognize Jacob, because his arms were hairy like Esau's. He was about to give him his blessing, [24]but asked again, "Are you really Esau?"

---

[a]BEERSHEBA: This name in Hebrew means "Well of the Vow" or "Well of Seven" (see also 21.31).
26.26 Gn 21.22

"I am," he answered.

25Isaac said, "Bring me some of the meat. After I eat it, I will give you my blessing." Jacob brought it to him, and he also brought him some wine to drink. **26**Then his father said to him, "Come closer and kiss me, son." **27**As he came up to kiss him, Isaac smelled his clothes—so he gave him his blessing. He said, "The pleasant smell of my son is like the smell of a field which the LORD has blessed. **28**May God give you dew from heaven and make your fields fertile! May he give you plenty of grain and wine! **29**May nations be your servants, and may peoples bow down before you. May you rule over all your relatives, and may your mother's descendants bow down before you. May those who curse you be cursed, and may those who bless you be blessed."

Esau Begs for Isaac's Blessing

30Isaac finished giving his blessing, and as soon as Jacob left, his brother Esau came in from hunting. **31**He also cooked some tasty food and took it to his father. He said, "Please, father, sit up and eat some of the meat that I have brought you, so that you can give me your blessing."

He gave him his blessing. (27.27)

32"Who are you?" Isaac asked.

"Your older son Esau," he answered.

33Isaac began to tremble and shake all over, and he asked, "Who was it, then, who killed an animal and brought it to me? I ate it just before you came. I gave him my final blessing, and so it is his forever."

34When Esau heard this, he cried out loudly and bitterly and said, "Give me your blessing also, father!"

35Isaac answered, "Your brother came and deceived me. He has taken away your blessing."

36Esau said, "This is the second time that he has cheated me. No wonder his name is Jacob.[a] He took my rights as the first-born son, and now he has taken away my blessing. Haven't you saved a blessing for me?"

37Isaac answered, "I have already made him master over you, and I have made all his relatives his slaves. I have given him grain and wine. Now there is nothing that I can do for you, son!"

38Esau continued to plead with his father: "Do you have only one blessing, father? Bless me too, father!" He began to cry.

39Then Isaac said to him,

"No dew from heaven for you,
    No fertile fields for you.
40You will live by your sword,
    But you will be your brother's slave.
Yet when you rebel,[b]
    You will break away from his control."

41Esau hated Jacob, because his father had given Jacob the blessing. He thought, "The time to mourn my father's death is near; then I will kill Jacob."

42But when Rebecca heard about Esau's plan, she sent for Jacob and said, "Listen, your brother Esau is planning to get even with you and kill you. **43**Now, son, do what I say. Go at once to my brother Laban in Haran, **44**and stay with him for a while, until your brother's anger

---

[a]JACOB: *This name sounds like the Hebrew for "cheat."*   [b]rebel; *or* grow restless.
27.27-29 He 11.20   **27.29** Gn 12.3   **27.36** Gn 25.29-34   **27.38** He 12.17   **27.39, 40** He 11.20
27.40 Gn 36.8; 2 K 8.20   **27.42** Ws 10.10

cools down 45and he forgets what you have done to him. Then I will send someone to bring you back. Why should I lose both of my sons on the same day?"

Isaac Sends Jacob to Laban

46Rebecca said to Isaac, "I am sick and tired of Esau's foreign wives. If Jacob also marries one of these Hittites, I might as well die."

28 Isaac called Jacob, greeted him, and told him, "Don't marry a Canaanite. 2Go instead to Mesopotamia, to the home of your grandfather Bethuel, and marry one of the young women there, one of your uncle Laban's daughters. 3May Almighty God bless your marriage and give you many children, so that you will become the father of many nations! 4May he bless you and your descendants as he blessed Abraham, and may you take possession of this land, in which you have lived and which God gave to Abraham!" 5Isaac sent Jacob away to Mesopotamia, to Laban, who was the son of Bethuel the Aramean and the brother of Rebecca, the mother of Jacob and Esau.

Esau Takes Another Wife

6Esau learned that Isaac had blessed Jacob and sent him away to Mesopotamia to find a wife. He also learned that when Isaac blessed him, he commanded him not to marry a Canaanite woman. 7He found out that Jacob had obeyed his father and mother and had gone to Mesopotamia. 8Esau then understood that his father Isaac did not approve of Canaanite women. 9So he went to Ishmael son of Abraham and married his daughter Mahalath, who was the sister of Nebaioth.

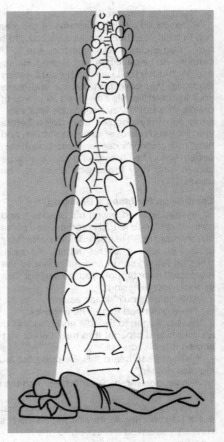

A stairway reaching from earth to heaven (28.12)

Jacob's Dream at Bethel

10Jacob left Beersheba and started toward Haran. 11At sunset he came to a holy place[a] and camped there. He lay down to sleep, resting his head on a stone. 12He dreamed that he saw a stairway reaching from earth to heaven, with angels going up and coming down on it. 13And there was the LORD standing beside him.[b] "I am the LORD, the God of Abraham and Isaac," he said. "I will give to you and to your descendants this land on which you are lying. 14They will be as numerous as the specks of dust on the earth. They will extend their territory in all directions, and through you and your descendants I will bless all the nations.[c] 15Remember, I will be with you and protect you wherever you go, and I will bring you back to this land. I will not leave you until I have done all that I have promised you."

16Jacob woke up and said, "The LORD is here! He is in this place, and I didn't know it!" 17He was afraid and said, "What a terrifying place this is! It must be the house of God; it must be the gate that opens into heaven."

18Jacob got up early next morning, took the stone that was under his head, and set it up

*a a holy place; *or* a place.   *b beside him; *or* on it.   *c through you . . . nations; *or* all the nations will ask me to bless them as I have blessed you and your descendants.
28.4 Gn 17.4-8   **28.10** Ws 10.10   **28.12** Jn 1.51   **28.13** Gn 13.14, 15   **28.14** Gn 12.3; 22.18

as a memorial. Then he poured olive oil on it to dedicate it to God. [19]He named the place Bethel.[a] (The town there was once known as Luz.) [20]Then Jacob made a vow to the LORD: "If you will be with me and protect me on the journey I am making and give me food and clothing, [21]and if I return safely to my father's home, then you will be my God. [22]This memorial stone which I have set up will be the place where you are worshiped, and I will give you a tenth of everything you give me."

Jacob Arrives at Laban's Home

29 Jacob continued on his way and went toward the land of the East. [2]Suddenly he came upon a well out in the fields with three flocks of sheep lying around it. The flocks were watered from this well, which had a large stone over the opening. [3]Whenever all the flocks came together there, the shepherds would roll the stone back and water them. Then they would put the stone back in place.

[4]Jacob asked the shepherds, "My friends, where are you from?"

"From Haran," they answered.

[5]He asked, "Do you know Laban, grandson of Nahor?"

"Yes, we do," they answered.

[6]"Is he well?" he asked.

"He is well," they answered. "Look, here comes his daughter Rachel with his flock."

[7]Jacob said, "Since it is still broad daylight and not yet time to bring the flocks in, why don't you water them and take them back to pasture?"

[8]They answered, "We can't do that until all the flocks are here and the stone has been rolled back; then we will water the flocks."

[9]While Jacob was still talking with them, Rachel arrived with the flock. [10]When Jacob saw Rachel with his uncle Laban's flock, he went to the well, rolled the stone back, and watered the sheep. [11]Then he kissed her and began to cry for joy. [12]He told her, "I am your father's relative, the son of Rebecca."

She ran to tell her father; [13]and when he heard the news about his nephew Jacob, he ran to meet him, hugged him and kissed him, and brought him into the house. When Jacob told Laban everything that had happened, [14]Laban said, "Yes, indeed, you are my own flesh and blood." Jacob stayed there a whole month.

Jacob Serves Laban for Rachel and Leah

[15]Laban said to Jacob, "You shouldn't work for me for nothing just because you are my relative. How much pay do you want?" [16]Laban had two daughters; the older was named Leah, and the younger Rachel. [17]Leah had lovely[b] eyes, but Rachel was shapely and beautiful.

[18]Jacob was in love with Rachel, so he said, "I will work seven years for you, if you will let me marry Rachel."

[19]Laban answered, "I would rather give her to you than to anyone else; stay here with me." [20]Jacob worked seven years so that he could have Rachel, and the time seemed like only a few days to him, because he loved her.

[21]Then Jacob said to Laban, "The time is up; let me marry your daughter." [22]So Laban gave a wedding feast and invited everyone. [23]But that night, instead of Rachel, he took Leah to Jacob, and Jacob had intercourse with her. ([24]Laban gave his slave woman Zilpah to his daughter Leah as her maid.) [25]Not until the next morning did Jacob discover that it was Leah. He went to Laban and said, "Why did you do this to me? I worked to get Rachel. Why have you tricked me?"

[26]Laban answered, "It is not the custom here to give the younger daughter in marriage before the older. [27]Wait until the week's marriage celebrations are over, and I will give you Rachel, if you will work for me another seven years."

[28]Jacob agreed, and when the week of marriage celebrations was over, Laban gave him his daughter Rachel as his wife. ([29]Laban gave his slave woman Bilhah to his daughter Rachel as her maid.) [30]Jacob had intercourse with Rachel also, and he loved her more than Leah. Then he worked for Laban another seven years.

[a]BETHEL: *This name in Hebrew means "house of God."*   [b]lovely; *or* weak.

The Children Born to Jacob

31When the LORD saw that Leah was loved less than Rachel, he made it possible for her to have children, but Rachel remained childless. **32**Leah became pregnant and gave birth to a son. She said, "The LORD has seen my trouble, and now my husband will love me"; so she named him Reuben.*a* **33**She became pregnant again and gave birth to another son. She said, "The LORD has given me this son also, because he heard that I was not loved"; so she named him Simeon.*b* **34**Once again she became pregnant and gave birth to another son. She said, "Now my husband will be bound more tightly to me, because I have borne him three sons"; so she named him Levi.*c* **35**Then she became pregnant again and gave birth to another son. She said, "This time I will praise the LORD"; so she named him Judah.*d* Then she stopped having children.

30 But Rachel had not borne Jacob any children, and so she became jealous of her sister and said to Jacob, "Give me children, or I will die."

2Jacob became angry with Rachel and said, "I can't take the place of God. He is the one who keeps you from having children."

3She said, "Here is my slave Bilhah; sleep with her, so that she can have a child for me. In this way I can become a mother through her." **4**So she gave Bilhah to her husband, and he had intercourse with her. **5**Bilhah became pregnant and bore Jacob a son. **6**Rachel said, "God has judged in my favor. He has heard my prayer and has given me a son"; so she named him Dan.*e* **7**Bilhah became pregnant again and bore Jacob a second son. **8**Rachel said, "I have fought a hard fight with my sister, but I have won"; so she named him Naphtali.*f*

9When Leah realized that she had stopped having children, she gave her slave Zilpah to Jacob as his wife. **10**Then Zilpah bore Jacob a son. **11**Leah said, "I have been lucky"; so she named him Gad.*g* **12**Zilpah bore Jacob another son, **13**and Leah said, "How happy I am! Now women will call me happy"; so she named him Asher.*h*

14During the wheat harvest Reuben went into the fields and found mandrakes,*i* which he brought to his mother Leah. Rachel said to Leah, "Please give me some of your son's mandrakes."

15Leah answered, "Isn't it enough that you have taken away my husband? Now you are even trying to take away my son's mandrakes."

Rachel said, "If you will give me your son's mandrakes, you can sleep with Jacob tonight."

16When Jacob came in from the fields in the evening, Leah went out to meet him and said, "You are going to sleep with me tonight, because I have paid for you with my son's mandrakes." So he had intercourse with her that night.

17God answered Leah's prayer, and she became pregnant and bore Jacob a fifth son. **18**Leah said, "God has given me my reward, because I gave my slave to my husband"; so she named her son Issachar.*j* **19**Leah became pregnant again and bore Jacob a sixth son. **20**She said, "God has given me a fine gift. Now my husband will accept me, because I have borne him six sons"; so she named him Zebulun.*k* **21**Later she bore a daughter, whom she named Dinah.

22Then God remembered Rachel; he answered her prayer and made it possible for her to have children. **23**She became pregnant and gave birth to a son. She said, "God has taken away my disgrace by giving me a son. **24**May the LORD give me another son"; so she named him Joseph.*l*

Jacob's Bargain with Laban

25After the birth of Joseph, Jacob said to Laban, "Let me go, so that I can return home. **26**Give me my wives and children that I have earned by working for you, and I will leave. You know how well I have served you."

---

*a*REUBEN: *This name sounds like the Hebrew for "see, a son" and "has seen my trouble."*   *b*SIMEON: *This name sounds like the Hebrew for "hear."*   *c*LEVI: *This name sounds like the Hebrew for "bound."*   *d*JUDAH: *This name sounds like the Hebrew for "praise."*   *e*DAN: *This name sounds like the Hebrew for "judge in favor."*   *f*NAPHTALI: *This name sounds like the Hebrew for "fight."*   *g*GAD: *This name in Hebrew means "luck."*   *h*ASHER: *This name in Hebrew means "happy."*   *i*MANDRAKES: *Plants which were believed to produce fertility and were used as love charms.*   *j*ISSACHAR: *This name sounds like the Hebrew for "a man is hired" and "there is reward."*   *k*ZEBULUN: *This name sounds like the Hebrew for "accept" and "gift."*   *l*JOSEPH: *This name sounds like the Hebrew for "may he give another" and "he has taken away."*

²⁷Laban said to him, "Let me say this: I have learned by divination that the LORD has blessed me because of you. ²⁸Name your wages, and I will pay them."

²⁹Jacob answered, "You know how I have worked for you and how your flocks have prospered under my care. ³⁰The little you had before I came has grown enormously, and the LORD has blessed you wherever I went.ᵃ Now it is time for me to look out for my own interests."

³¹"What shall I pay you?" Laban asked.

Jacob answered, "I don't want any wages. I will continue to take care of your flocks if you agree to this suggestion: ³²Let me go through all your flocks today and take every black lambᵇ and every spotted or speckled young goat. That is all the wages I want. ³³In the future you can easily find out if I have been honest. When you come to check up on my wages, if I have any goat that isn't speckled or spotted or any sheep that isn't black, you will know that it has been stolen."

³⁴Laban answered, "Agreed. We will do as you suggest." ³⁵But that day Laban removed the male goats that had stripes or spots and all the females that were speckled and spotted or which had white on them; he also removed all the black sheep. He put his sons in charge of them, ³⁶and then went away from Jacob with this flock as far as he could travel in three days. Jacob took care of the rest of Laban's flocks.

³⁷Jacob got green branches of poplar, almond, and plane trees and stripped off some of the bark so that the branches had white stripes on them. ³⁸He placed these branches in front of the flocks at their drinking troughs. He put them there, because the animals mated when they came to drink. ³⁹So when the goats bred in front of the branches, they produced young that were streaked, speckled, and spotted.

⁴⁰Jacob kept the sheep separate from the goats and made them face in the direction of the streaked and black animals of Laban's flock. In this way he built up his own flock and kept it apart from Laban's.

⁴¹When the healthy animals were mating, Jacob put the branches in front of them at the drinking troughs, so that they would breed among the branches. ⁴²But he did not put the branches in front of the weak animals. Soon Laban had all the weak animals, and Jacob all the healthy ones. ⁴³In this way Jacob became very wealthy. He had many flocks, slaves, camels, and donkeys.

Jacob Flees from Laban

31 Jacob heard that Laban's sons were saying, "Jacob has taken everything that belonged to our father. He got all his wealth from what our father owned." ²He also saw that Laban was no longer as friendly as he had been earlier. ³Then the LORD said to him, "Go back to the land of your fathers and to your relatives. I will be with you."

⁴So Jacob sent word to Rachel and Leah to meet him in the field where his flocks were. ⁵He said to them, "I have noticed that your father is not as friendly toward me as he used to be; but my father's God has been with me. ⁶You both know that I have worked for your father with all my strength. ⁷Yet he has cheated me and changed my wages ten times. But God did not let him harm me. ⁸Whenever Laban said, 'The speckled goats shall be your wages,' all the flocks produced speckled young. When he said, 'The striped goats shall be your wages,' all the flocks produced striped young. ⁹God has taken flocks away from your father and given them to me.

¹⁰"During the breeding season I had a dream, and I saw that the male goats that were mating were striped, spotted, and speckled. ¹¹The angel of God spoke to me in the dream and said, 'Jacob!' 'Yes,' I answered. ¹²'Look,' he continued, 'all the male goats that are mating are striped, spotted, and speckled. I am making this happen because I have seen all that Laban is doing to you. ¹³I am the God who appeared to you at Bethel, where you dedicated a stone as a memorial by pouring olive oil on it and where you made a vow to me. Now get ready and go back to the land where you were born.' "

¹⁴Rachel and Leah answered Jacob, "There is nothing left for us to inherit from our father. ¹⁵He treats us like foreigners. He sold us, and now he has spent all the money he was

---

ᵃwherever I went; or because of me.   ᵇOne ancient translation every black lamb; Hebrew every spotted and speckled lamb, and every black lamb.
31.13 Gn 28.18-22

paid for us. ¹⁶All this wealth which God has taken from our father belongs to us and to our children. Do whatever God has told you."

¹⁷⁻¹⁸So Jacob got ready to go back to his father in the land of Canaan. He put his children and his wives on the camels, and drove all his flocks ahead of him, with everything that he had gotten in Mesopotamia. ¹⁹Laban had gone to shear his sheep, and during his absence Rachel stole the household gods that belonged to her father. ²⁰Jacob deceived Laban by not letting him know that he was leaving. ²¹He took everything he owned and left in a hurry. He crossed the Euphrates River and started for the hill country of Gilead.

Laban Pursues Jacob

²²Three days later Laban was told that Jacob had fled. ²³He took his men with him and pursued Jacob for seven days until he caught up with him in the hill country of Gilead. ²⁴In a dream that night God came to Laban and said to him, "Be careful not to threaten Jacob in any way." ²⁵Jacob had set up his camp on a mountain, and Laban set up his camp with his relatives in the hill country of Gilead.

²⁶Laban said to Jacob, "Why did you deceive me and carry off my daughters like women captured in war? ²⁷Why did you deceive me and slip away without telling me? If you had told me, I would have sent you on your way with rejoicing and singing to the music of tambourines and harps. ²⁸You did not even let me kiss my grandchildren and my daughters good-bye. That was a foolish thing to do! ²⁹I have the power to do you harm, but last night the God of your father warned me not to threaten you in any way. ³⁰I know that you left because you were so anxious to get back home, but why did you steal my household gods?"

³¹Jacob answered, "I was afraid, because I thought that you might take your daughters away from me. ³²But if you find that anyone here has your gods, he will be put to death. Here, with our men as witnesses, look for anything that belongs to you and take what is yours." Jacob did not know that Rachel had stolen Laban's gods.

³³Laban went and searched Jacob's tent; then he went into Leah's tent, and the tent of the two slave women, but he did not find his gods. Then he went into Rachel's tent. ³⁴Rachel had taken the household gods and put them in a camel's saddlebag and was sitting on them. Laban searched through the whole tent, but did not find them. ³⁵Rachel said to her father, "Do not be angry with me, sir, but I am not able to stand up in your presence; I am having my monthly period." Laban searched but did not find his household gods.

³⁶Then Jacob lost his temper. "What crime have I committed?" he asked angrily. "What law have I broken that gives you the right to hunt me down? ³⁷Now that you have searched through all my belongings, what household article have you found that belongs to you? Put it out here where your men and mine can see it, and let them decide which one of us is right. ³⁸I have been with you now for twenty years; your sheep and your goats have not failed to reproduce, and I have not eaten any rams from your flocks. ³⁹Whenever a sheep was killed by wild animals, I always bore the loss myself. I didn't take it to you to show that it was not my fault. You demanded that I make good anything that was stolen during the day or during the night. ⁴⁰Many times I suffered from the heat during the day and from the cold at night. I was not able to sleep. ⁴¹It was like that for the whole twenty years I was with you. For fourteen years I worked to win your two daughters—and six years for your flocks. And even then, you changed my wages ten times. ⁴²If the God of my fathers, the God of Abraham and Isaac, had not been with me, you would have already sent me away empty-handed. But God has seen my trouble and the work I have done, and last night he gave his judgment."

The Agreement between Jacob and Laban

⁴³Laban answered Jacob, "These young women are my daughters; their children belong to me, and these flocks are mine. In fact, everything you see here belongs to me. But since I can do nothing to keep my daughters and their children, ⁴⁴I am ready to make an agreement with you. Let us make a pile of stones to remind us of our agreement."

⁴⁵So Jacob got a stone and set it up as a memorial. ⁴⁶He told his men to gather some rocks and pile them up. Then they ate a meal beside the pile of rocks. ⁴⁷Laban named it Jegar Sahadutha,ᵃ while Jacob named it Galeed.ᵇ ⁴⁸Laban said to Jacob, "This pile of rocks

---

ᵃJEGAR SAHADUTHA: *This name in Aramaic means "a pile to remind us."*   ᵇGALEED: *This name in Hebrew means "a pile to remind us."*

Jacob drove all his flocks ahead of him. (31.18)

will be a reminder for both of us." That is why that place was named Galeed. ⁴⁹Laban also said, "May the LORD keep an eye on us while we are separated from each other." So the place was also named Mizpah.ᵃ ⁵⁰Laban went on, "If you mistreat my daughters or if you marry other women, even though I don't know about it, remember that God is watching us. ⁵¹Here are the rocks that I have piled up between us, and here is the memorial stone. ⁵²Both this pile and this memorial stone are reminders. I will never go beyond this pile to attack you, and you must never go beyond it or beyond this memorial stone to attack me. ⁵³The God of Abraham and the God of Nahorᵇ will judge between us." Then, in the name of the God whom his father Isaac worshiped, Jacob solemnly vowed to keep this promise. ⁵⁴He killed an animal, which he offered as a sacrifice on the mountain, and he invited his men to the meal. After they had eaten, they spent the night on the mountain. ⁵⁵Early the next morning Laban kissed his grandchildren and his daughters good-bye, and left to go back home.

Jacob Prepares to Meet Esau

32 As Jacob went on his way, some angels met him. ²When he saw them, he said, "This is God's camp"; so he named the place Mahanaim.ᶜ

³Jacob sent messengers ahead of him to his brother Esau in the country of Edom. ⁴He instructed them to say: "I, Jacob, your obedient servant, report to my master Esau that I have been staying with Laban and that I have delayed my return until now. ⁵I own cattle, donkeys, sheep, goats, and slaves. I am sending you word, sir, in the hope of gaining your favor."

⁶When the messengers came back to Jacob, they said, "We went to your brother Esau, and he is already on his way to meet you. He has four hundred men with him." ⁷Jacob was frightened and worried. He divided into two groups the people who were with him, and also his sheep, goats, cattle, and camels. ⁸He thought, "If Esau comes and attacks the first group, the other may be able to escape."

⁹Then Jacob prayed, "God of my grandfather Abraham and God of my father Isaac, hear me! You told me, LORD, to go back to my land and to my relatives, and you would make everything go well for me. ¹⁰I am not worth all the kindness and faithfulness that you have shown me, your servant. I crossed the Jordan with nothing but a walking stick, and now I have come back with these two groups. ¹¹Save me, I pray, from my brother Esau. I am afraid—afraid that he is coming to attack us and destroy us all, even the women and children. ¹²Remember that you promised to make everything go well for me and to give me more descendants than anyone could count, as many as the grains of sand along the seashore."

ᵃMIZPAH: *This name sounds like the Hebrew for "place from which to watch."*   ᵇABRAHAM . . . NAHOR: *Abraham was Jacob's grandfather and Nahor was Laban's grandfather.*   ᶜMAHANAIM: *This name in Hebrew means "two camps."*
32.12 Gn 22.17

13-15After spending the night there, Jacob chose from his livestock as a present for his brother Esau: 200 female goats and 20 males, 200 female sheep and 20 males, 30 milk camels with their young, 40 cows and 10 bulls, 20 female donkeys and 10 males. 16He divided them into herds and put one of his servants in charge of each herd. He said to them, "Go ahead of me, and leave a space between each herd and the one behind it." 17He ordered the first servant, "When my brother Esau meets you and asks, 'Who is your master? Where are you going? Who owns these animals in front of you?' 18you must answer, 'They belong to your servant Jacob. He sends them as a present to his master Esau. Jacob himself is right behind us.' " 19He gave the same order to the second, the third, and to all the others who were in charge of the herds: "This is what you must say to Esau when you meet him. 20You must say, 'Yes, your servant Jacob is right behind us.' " Jacob was thinking, "I will win him over with the gifts, and when I meet him, perhaps he will forgive me." 21He sent the gifts on ahead of him and spent that night in camp.

Jacob Wrestles at Peniel

22That same night Jacob got up, took his two wives, his two concubines, and his eleven children, and crossed the Jabbok River. 23After he had sent them across, he also sent across all that he owned, 24but he stayed behind, alone.

Then a man came and wrestled with him until just before daybreak. 25When the man saw that he was not winning the struggle, he hit Jacob on the hip, and it was thrown out of joint. 26The man said, "Let me go; daylight is coming."

"I won't, unless you bless me," Jacob answered.

27"What is your name?" the man asked.

"Jacob," he answered.

28The man said, "Your name will no longer be Jacob. You have struggled with God and with men, and you have won; so your name will be Israel."a

29Jacob said, "Now tell me your name."

But he answered, "Why do you want to know my name?" Then he blessed Jacob.

A man came and wrestled with him. (32.24)

30Jacob said, "I have seen God face to face, and I am still alive"; so he named the place Peniel.b 31The sun rose as Jacob was leaving Peniel, and he was limping because of his hip. 32Even today the descendants of Israel do not eat the muscle which is on the hip joint, because it was on this muscle that Jacob was hit.

Jacob Meets Esau

33 Jacob saw Esau coming with his four hundred men, so he divided the children among Leah, Rachel, and the two concubines. 2He put the concubines and their children first, then Leah and her children, and finally Rachel and Joseph at the rear. 3Jacob went ahead of them and bowed down to the ground seven times as he approached his brother. 4But Esau ran to meet him, threw his arms around him, and kissed him. They were both crying. 5When Esau looked around and saw the women and the children, he asked, "Who are these people with you?"

"These, sir, are the children whom God has been good enough to give me," Jacob answered. 6Then the concubines came up with their children and bowed down; 7then Leah and her children came, and last of all Joseph and Rachel came and bowed down.

8Esau asked, "What about that other group I met? What did that mean?"

Jacob answered, "It was to gain your favor."

aISRAEL: *This name sounds like the Hebrew for "he struggles with God" or "God struggles."*   bPENIEL: *This name sounds like the Hebrew for "the face of God."*
32.23 Ws 10.12   **32.24-26** Ho 12.3, 4   **32.28** Gn 35.10   **32.29** Jg 13.17, 18

Esau . . . threw his arms around him. (33.4)

⁹But Esau said, "I have enough, my brother; keep what you have."

¹⁰Jacob said, "No, please, if I have gained your favor, accept my gift. To see your face is for me like seeing the face of God, now that you have been so friendly to me. ¹¹Please accept this gift which I have brought for you; God has been kind to me and given me everything I need." Jacob kept on urging him until he accepted.

¹²Esau said, "Let's get ready and leave. I will go ahead of you."

¹³Jacob answered, "You know that the children are weak, and I must think of the sheep and livestock with their young. If they are driven hard for even one day, the whole herd will die. ¹⁴Please go on ahead of me, and I will follow slowly, going as fast as I can with the livestock and the children until I catch up with you in Edom."

¹⁵Esau said, "Then let me leave some of my men with you."

But Jacob answered, "There is no need for that for I only want to gain your favor."ᵃ ¹⁶So that day Esau started on his way back to Edom. ¹⁷But Jacob went to Sukkoth, where he built a house for himself and shelters for his livestock. That is why the place was named Sukkoth.ᵇ

¹⁸On his return from Mesopotamia Jacob arrived safely at the city of Shechem in the land of Canaan and set up his camp in a field near the city. ¹⁹He bought that part of the field from the descendants of Hamor father of Shechem for a hundred pieces of silver. ²⁰He put up an altar there and named it for El, the God of Israel.

ᵃfor I only want to gain your favor; *or* if it's all right with you.   ᵇSUKKOTH: *This name in Hebrew means* "shelters."

33.19 Js 24.32; Jn 4.5

The Rape of Dinah

34 One day Dinah, the daughter of Jacob and Leah, went to visit some of the Canaanite women. [2]When Shechem son of Hamor the Hivite, who was chief of that region, saw her, he took her and raped her. [3]But he found the young woman so attractive that he fell in love with her and tried to win her affection.[a] [4]He told his father, "I want you to get Dinah for me as my wife."

[5]Jacob learned that his daughter had been disgraced, but because his sons were out in the fields with his livestock, he did nothing until they came back. [6]Shechem's father Hamor went out to talk with Jacob, [7]just as Jacob's sons were coming in from the fields. When they heard about it, they were shocked and furious that Shechem had done such a thing and had insulted the people of Israel by raping Jacob's daughter. [8]Hamor said to him, "My son Shechem has fallen in love with your daughter; please let him marry her. [9]Let us make an agreement that there will be intermarriage between our people and yours. [10]Then you may stay here in our country with us; you may live anywhere you wish, trade freely, and own property."

[11]Then Shechem said to Dinah's father and brothers, "Do me this favor, and I will give you whatever you want. [12]Tell me what presents you want, and set the payment for the bride as high as you wish; I will give you whatever you ask, if you will only let me marry her."

[13]Because Shechem had disgraced their sister Dinah, Jacob's sons answered Shechem and his father Hamor in a deceitful way. [14]They said to him, "We cannot let our sister marry a man who is not circumcised; that would be a disgrace for us. [15]We can agree only on the condition that you become like us by circumcising all your males. [16]Then we will agree to intermarriage. We will settle among you and become one people with you. [17]But if you will not accept our terms and be circumcised, we will take her and leave."

[18]These terms seemed fair to Hamor and his son Shechem, [19]and the young man lost no time in doing what was suggested, because he was in love with Jacob's daughter. He was the most important member of his family.

[20]Hamor and his son Shechem went to the meeting place at the city gate and spoke to the people of the town: [21]"These men are friendly; let them live in the land with us and travel freely. The land is large enough for them also. Let us marry their daughters and give them ours in marriage. [22]But these men will agree to live among us and be one people with us only on the condition that we circumcise all our males, as they are circumcised. [23]Won't all their livestock and everything else they own be ours? So let us agree that they can live among us." [24]All the citizens of the city agreed with what Hamor and Shechem proposed, and all the males were circumcised.

[25]Three days later, when the men were still sore from their circumcision, two of Jacob's sons, Simeon and Levi, the brothers of Dinah, took their swords, went into the city without arousing suspicion, and killed all the men, [26]including Hamor and his son Shechem. Then they took Dinah from Shechem's house and left. [27]After the slaughter Jacob's other sons looted the town to take revenge for their sister's disgrace. [28]They took the flocks, the cattle, the donkeys, and everything else in the city and in the fields. [29]They took everything of value, captured all the women and children, and carried off everything in the houses.

[30]Jacob said to Simeon and Levi, "You have gotten me into trouble; now the Canaanites, the Perizzites, and everybody else in the land will hate me. I do not have many men; if they all band together against me and attack me, our whole family will be destroyed."

[31]But they answered, "We cannot let our sister be treated like a common whore."

God Blesses Jacob at Bethel

35 God said to Jacob, "Go to Bethel at once, and live there. Build an altar there to me, the God who appeared to you when you were running away from your brother Esau."

[2]So Jacob said to his family and to all who were with him, "Get rid of the foreign gods that you have; purify yourselves and put on clean clothes. [3]We are going to leave here and go to Bethel, where I will build an altar to the God who helped me in the time of my trouble and who has been with me everywhere I have gone." [4]So they gave Jacob all the foreign

---

[a]tried to win her affection; or comforted her.
35.1 Gn 28.11-17

gods that they had and also the earrings that they were wearing. He buried them beneath the oak tree near Shechem.

[5]When Jacob and his sons started to leave, great fear fell on the people of the nearby towns, and they did not pursue them. [6]Jacob came with all his people to Luz, which is now known as Bethel, in the land of Canaan. [7]He built an altar there and named the place for the God of Bethel, because God had revealed himself to him there when he was running away from his brother. [8]Rebecca's nurse Deborah died and was buried beneath the oak south of Bethel. So it was named "Oak of Weeping."

[9]When Jacob returned from Mesopotamia, God appeared to him again and blessed him. [10]God said to him, "Your name is Jacob, but from now on it will be Israel." So God named him Israel. [11]And God said to him, "I am Almighty God. Have many children. Nations will be descended from you, and you will be the ancestor of kings. [12]I will give you the land which I gave to Abraham and to Isaac, and I will also give it to your descendants after you." [13]Then God left him. [14]There, where God had spoken to him, Jacob set up a memorial stone and consecrated it by pouring wine and olive oil on it. [15]He named the place Bethel.

The Death of Rachel

[16]Jacob and his family left Bethel, and when they were still some distance from Ephrath, the time came for Rachel to have her baby, and she was having difficult labor. [17]When her labor pains were at their worst, the midwife said to her, "Don't be afraid, Rachel; it's another boy." [18]But she was dying, and as she breathed her last, she named her son Benoni,[a] but his father named him Benjamin.[b]

[19]When Rachel died, she was buried beside the road to Ephrath, now known as Bethlehem. [20]Jacob set up a memorial stone there, and it still marks Rachel's grave to this day. [21]Jacob moved on and set up his camp on the other side of the tower of Eder.

The Sons of Jacob
(1 Chronicles 2.1, 2)

[22]While Jacob was living in that land, Reuben had sexual intercourse with Bilhah, one of his father's concubines; Jacob heard about it and was furious.[c]

Jacob had twelve sons. [23]The sons of Leah were Reuben (Jacob's oldest son), Simeon, Levi, Judah, Issachar, and Zebulun. [24]The sons of Rachel were Joseph and Benjamin. [25]The sons of Rachel's slave Bilhah were Dan and Naphtali. [26]The sons of Leah's slave Zilpah were Gad and Asher. These sons were born in Mesopotamia.

The Death of Isaac

[27]Jacob went to his father Isaac at Mamre, near Hebron, where Abraham and Isaac had lived. [28]Isaac lived to be a hundred and eighty years old [29]and died at a ripe old age; and his sons Esau and Jacob buried him.

The Descendants of Esau
(1 Chronicles 1.34-37)

36 These are the descendants of Esau, also called Edom. [2]Esau married Canaanite women: Adah, the daughter of Elon the Hittite; Oholibamah, the daughter of Anah son[d] of Zibeon the Hivite; [3]and Basemath, the daughter of Ishmael and sister of Nebaioth. [4]Adah bore Eliphaz; Basemath bore Reuel; [5]and Oholibamah bore Jeush, Jalam, and Korah. All these sons were born to Esau in the land of Canaan.

[6]Then Esau took his wives, his sons, his daughters, and all the people of his house, along with all his livestock and all the possessions he had gotten in the land of Canaan, and went away from his brother Jacob to another land. [7]He left because the land where he and Jacob were living was not able to support them; they had too much livestock and could no longer stay together. [8]So Esau lived in the hill country of Edom.

[9]These are the descendants of Esau, the ancestor of the Edomites. [10-13]Esau's wife Adah

---

[a]BENONI: *This name in Hebrew means "son of my sorrow."*   [b]BENJAMIN: *This name in Hebrew means "son who will be fortunate."*   [c]One ancient translation *and was furious;* Hebrew *does not have these words.*   [d]Some ancient translations *son;* Hebrew *daughter; or* granddaughter.
35.10 Gn 32.28   **35.11, 12** Gn 17.4-8   **35.14, 15** Gn 28.18, 19   **35.22** Gn 49.4   **35.27** Gn 13.18
36.2 Gn 26.34   **36.3** Gn 28.9

bore him one son, Eliphaz, and Eliphaz had five sons: Teman, Omar, Zepho, Gatam, and Kenaz. And by another wife, Timna, he had one more son, Amalek.

Esau's wife Basemath bore him one son, Reuel, and Reuel had four sons: Nahath, Zerah, Shammah, and Mizzah.

¹⁴Esau's wife Oholibamah, the daughter of Anah son*a* of Zibeon, bore him three sons: Jeush, Jalam, and Korah.

¹⁵These are the tribes descended from Esau. Esau's first son Eliphaz was the ancestor of the following tribes: Teman, Omar, Zepho, Kenaz, ¹⁶Korah, Gatam, and Amalek. These were all descendants of Esau's wife Adah.

¹⁷Esau's son Reuel was the ancestor of the following tribes: Nahath, Zerah, Shammah, and Mizzah. These were all descendants of Esau's wife Basemath.

¹⁸The following tribes were descended from Esau by his wife Oholibamah, the daughter of Anah: Jeush, Jalam, and Korah. ¹⁹All these tribes were descended from Esau.

The Descendants of Seir
(1 Chronicles 1.38-42)

²⁰⁻²¹The original inhabitants of the land of Edom were divided into tribes which traced their ancestry to the following descendants of Seir, a Horite: Lotan, Shobal, Zibeon, Anah, Dishon, Ezer, and Dishan.

²²Lotan was the ancestor of the clans of Hori and Heman. (Lotan had a sister named Timna.)

²³Shobal was the ancestor of the clans of Alvan, Manahath, Ebal, Shepho, and Onam.

²⁴Zibeon had two sons, Aiah and Anah. (This is the Anah who found the hot springs in the wilderness when he was taking care of his father's donkeys.) ²⁵⁻²⁶Anah was the father of Dishon, who was the ancestor of the clans of Hemdan, Eshban, Ithran, and Cheran. Anah also had a daughter named Oholibamah.

²⁷Ezer was the ancestor of the clans of Bilhan, Zaavan, and Akan.

²⁸Dishan was the ancestor of the clans of Uz and Aran.

²⁹⁻³⁰These are the Horite tribes in the land of Edom: Lotan, Shobal, Zibeon, Anah, Dishon, Ezer, and Dishan.

The Kings of Edom
(1 Chronicles 1.43-54)

³¹⁻³⁹Before there were any kings in Israel, the following kings ruled the land of Edom in succession:

Bela son of Beor from Dinhabah
Jobab son of Zerah from Bozrah
Husham from the region of Teman
Hadad son of Bedad from Avith (he defeated the Midianites in a battle in the country of Moab)
Samlah from Masrekah
Shaul from Rehoboth-on-the-River
Baal Hanan son of Achbor
Hadad from Pau (his wife was Mehetabel, the daughter of Matred and granddaughter of Mezahab)

⁴⁰⁻⁴³Esau was the ancestor of the following Edomite tribes: Timna, Alvah, Jetheth, Oholibamah, Elah, Pinon, Kenaz, Teman, Mibzar, Magdiel, and Iram. The area where each of these tribes lived was known by the name of the tribe.

Joseph and His Brothers

37 Jacob continued to live in the land of Canaan, where his father had lived, ²and this is the story of Jacob's family.

Joseph, a young man of seventeen, took care of the sheep and goats with his brothers, the sons of Bilhah and Zilpah, his father's concubines. He brought bad reports to his father about what his brothers were doing.

³Jacob loved Joseph more than all his other sons, because he had been born to him when

---

aSome ancient translations son; *Hebrew* daughter; *or* granddaughter.

HIGHLIGHTS IN JOSEPH'S LIFE (37—46)
(Numbers refer to chapter and verse in Genesis)

he was old. He made a long robe with full sleeves[a] for him. 4When his brothers saw that their father loved Joseph more than he loved them, they hated their brother so much that they would not speak to him in a friendly manner.

5One time Joseph had a dream, and when he told his brothers about it, they hated him even more. 6He said, "Listen to the dream I had. 7We were all in the field tying up sheaves of wheat, when my sheaf got up and stood up straight. Yours formed a circle around mine and bowed down to it."

8"Do you think you are going to be a king and rule over us?" his brothers asked. So they hated him even more because of his dreams and because of what he said about them.

9Then Joseph had another dream and told his brothers, "I had another dream, in which I saw the sun, the moon, and eleven stars bowing down to me."

10He also told the dream to his father, and his father scolded him: "What kind of a dream is that? Do you think that your mother, your brothers, and I are going to come and bow down to you?" 11Joseph's brothers were jealous of him, but his father kept thinking about the whole matter.

Joseph Is Sold and Taken to Egypt

12One day when Joseph's brothers had gone to Shechem to take care of their father's flock, 13Jacob said to Joseph, "I want you to go to Shechem, where your brothers are taking care of the flock."

Joseph answered, "I am ready."

14His father told him, "Go and see if your brothers are safe and if the flock is all right; then come back and tell me." So his father sent him on his way from Hebron Valley.

Joseph arrived at Shechem 15and was wandering around in the country when a man saw him and asked him, "What are you looking for?"

16"I am looking for my brothers, who are taking care of their flock," he answered. "Can you tell me where they are?"

17The man said, "They have already left. I heard them say that they were going to Dothan." So Joseph went after his brothers and found them at Dothan.

18They saw him in the distance, and before he reached them, they plotted against him and decided to kill him. 19They said to one another, "Here comes that dreamer. 20Come on now, let's kill him and throw his body into one of the dry wells. We can say that a wild animal killed him. Then we will see what becomes of his dreams."

21Reuben heard them and tried to save Joseph. "Let's not kill him," he said. 22"Just throw him into this well in the wilderness, but don't hurt him." He said this, planning to save him from them and send him back to his father. 23When Joseph came up to his brothers, they ripped off his long robe with full sleeves.[a] 24Then they took him and threw him into the well, which was dry.

25While they were eating, they suddenly saw a group of Ishmaelites traveling from Gilead to Egypt. Their camels were loaded with spices and resins. 26Judah said to his brothers, "What will we gain by killing our brother and covering up the murder? 27Let's sell him to these Ishmaelites. Then we won't have to hurt him; after all, he is our brother, our own flesh and blood." His brothers agreed, 28and when some Midianite traders came by, the brothers[b] pulled Joseph out of the well and sold him for twenty pieces of silver to the Ishmaelites, who took him to Egypt.

29When Reuben came back to the well and found that Joseph was not there, he tore his clothes in sorrow. 30He returned to his brothers and said, "The boy is not there! What am I going to do?"

31Then they killed a goat and dipped Joseph's robe in its blood. 32They took the robe to their father and said, "We found this. Does it belong to your son?"

33He recognized it and said, "Yes, it is his! Some wild animal has killed him. My son Joseph has been torn to pieces!" 34Jacob tore his clothes in sorrow and put on sackcloth. He mourned for his son a long time. 35All his sons and daughters came to comfort him, but he refused to be comforted and said, "I will go down to the world of the dead still mourning for my son." So he continued to mourn for his son Joseph.

---

[a]robe with full sleeves; or decorated robe.   [b]the brothers; Hebrew they.
37.11 Ac 7.9   **37.28** Ws 10.13; Ac 7.9

CREATION

"God looked at everything he had made,
and he was very pleased."

—*Genesis 1.31*

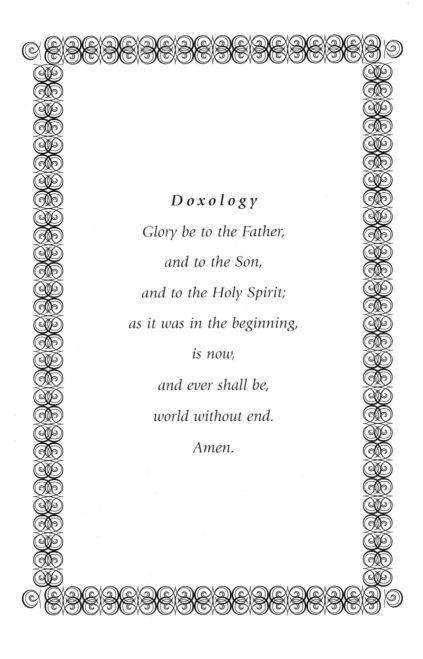

Doxology

Glory be to the Father,

and to the Son,

and to the Holy Spirit;

as it was in the beginning,

is now,

and ever shall be,

world without end.

Amen.

³⁶Meanwhile, in Egypt the Midianites had sold Joseph to Potiphar, one of the king's officers, who was the captain of the palace guard.

Judah and Tamar

38 About that time Judah left his brothers and went to stay with a man named Hirah, who was from the town of Adullam. ²There Judah met a young Canaanite woman whose father was named Shua. He married her, ³and she bore him a son, whom he named Er. ⁴She became pregnant again and bore another son and named him Onan. ⁵Again she had a son and named him Shelah. Judah was at Achzib when the boy was born.

⁶For his first son Er, Judah got a wife whose name was Tamar. ⁷Er's conduct was evil, and it displeased the LORD, so the LORD killed him. ⁸Then Judah said to Er's brother Onan, "Go and sleep with your brother's widow. Fulfill your obligation to her as her husband's brother, so that your brother may have descendants." ⁹But Onan knew that the children would not belong to him, so when he had intercourse with his brother's widow, he let the semen spill on the ground, so that there would be no children for his brother. ¹⁰What he did displeased the LORD, and the LORD killed him also. ¹¹Then Judah said to his daughter-in-law Tamar, "Return to your father's house and remain a widow until my son Shelah grows up." He said this because he was afraid that Shelah would be killed, as his brothers had been. So Tamar went back home.

¹²After some time Judah's wife died. When he had finished the time of mourning, he and his friend Hirah of Adullam went to Timnah, where his sheep were being sheared. ¹³Someone told Tamar that her father-in-law was going to Timnah to shear his sheep. ¹⁴So she changed from the widow's clothes she had been wearing, covered her face with a veil, and sat down at the entrance to Enaim, a town on the road to Timnah. As she well knew, Judah's youngest son Shelah was now grown up, and yet she had not been given to him in marriage.

¹⁵When Judah saw her, he thought that she was a prostitute, because she had her face covered. ¹⁶He went over to her at the side of the road and said, "All right, how much do you charge?" (He did not know that she was his daughter-in-law.)

She said, "What will you give me?"

¹⁷He answered, "I will send you a young goat from my flock."

She said, "All right, if you will give me something to keep as a pledge until you send the goat."

¹⁸"What shall I give you as a pledge?" he asked.

She answered, "Your seal with its cord and the walking stick you are carrying." He gave them to her. Then they had intercourse, and she became pregnant. ¹⁹Tamar went home, took off her veil, and put her widow's clothes back on.

²⁰Judah sent his friend Hirah to take the goat and get back from the woman the articles he had pledged, but Hirah could not find her. ²¹He asked some men at Enaim, "Where is the prostitute who was here by the road?"

"There has never been a prostitute here," they answered.

²²He returned to Judah and said, "I couldn't find her. The men of the place said that there had never been a prostitute there."

²³Judah said, "Let her keep the things. We don't want people to laugh at us. I did try to pay her, but you couldn't find her."

²⁴About three months later someone told Judah, "Your daughter-in-law Tamar has been acting like a whore, and now she is pregnant."

Judah ordered, "Take her out and burn her to death."

²⁵As she was being taken out, she sent word to her father-in-law: "I am pregnant by the man who owns these things. Look at them and see whose they are—this seal with its cord and this walking stick."

²⁶Judah recognized them and said, "She is in the right. I have failed in my obligation to her—I should have given her to my son Shelah in marriage." And Judah never had intercourse with her again.

²⁷When the time came for her to give birth, it was discovered that she was going to have twins. ²⁸While she was in labor, one of them put out an arm; the midwife caught it, tied a red thread around it, and said, "This one was born first." ²⁹But he pulled his arm back, and his

brother was born first. Then the midwife said, "So this is how you break your way out!" So he was named Perez.ᵃ ³⁰Then his brother was born with the red thread on his arm, and he was named Zerah.ᵇ

Joseph and Potiphar's Wife

39 Now the Ishmaelites had taken Joseph to Egypt and sold him to Potiphar, one of the king's officers, who was the captain of the palace guard. ²The LORD was with Joseph and made him successful. He lived in the house of his Egyptian master, ³who saw that the LORD was with Joseph and had made him successful in everything he did. ⁴Potiphar was pleased with him and made him his personal servant; so he put him in charge of his house and everything he owned. ⁵From then on, because of Joseph the LORD blessed the household of the Egyptian and everything that he had in his house and in his fields. ⁶Potiphar turned over everything he had to the care of Joseph and did not concern himself with anything except the food he ate.

Joseph was well-built and good-looking, ⁷and after a while his master's wife began to desire Joseph and asked him to go to bed with her. ⁸He refused and said to her, "Look, my master does not have to concern himself with anything in the house, because I am here. He has put me in charge of everything he has. ⁹I have as much authority in this house as he has, and he has not kept back anything from me except you. How then could I do such an immoral thing and sin against God?" ¹⁰Although she asked Joseph day after day, he would not go to bed with her.

¹¹But one day when Joseph went into the house to do his work, none of the house servants was there. ¹²She caught him by his robe and said, "Come to bed with me." But he escaped and ran outside, leaving his robe in her hand. ¹³When she saw that he had left his robe and had run out of the house, ¹⁴she called to her house servants and said, "Look at this! This Hebrew that my husband brought to the house is insulting us. He came into my room and tried to rape me, but I screamed as loud as I could. ¹⁵When he heard me scream, he ran outside, leaving his robe beside me."

¹⁶She kept his robe with her until Joseph's master came home. ¹⁷Then she told him the same story: "That Hebrew slave that you brought here came into my room and insulted me. ¹⁸But when I screamed, he ran outside, leaving his robe beside me."

¹⁹Joseph's master was furious ²⁰and had Joseph arrested and put in the prison where the king's prisoners were kept, and there he stayed. ²¹But the LORD was with Joseph and blessed him, so that the jailer was pleased with him. ²²He put Joseph in charge of all the other prisoners and made him responsible for everything that was done in the prison. ²³The jailer did not have to look after anything for which Joseph was responsible, because the LORD was with Joseph and made him succeed in everything he did.

Joseph Interprets the Prisoners' Dreams

40 Some time later the king of Egypt's wine steward and his chief baker offended the king. ²He was angry with these two officials ³and put them in prison in the house of the captain of the guard, in the same place where Joseph was being kept. ⁴They spent a long time in prison, and the captain assigned Joseph as their servant.

⁵One night there in prison the wine steward and the chief baker each had a dream, and the dreams had different meanings. ⁶When Joseph came to them in the morning, he saw that they were upset. ⁷He asked them, "Why do you look so worried today?"

⁸They answered, "Each of us had a dream, and there is no one here to explain what the dreams mean."

"It is God who gives the ability to interpret dreams," Joseph said. "Tell me your dreams."

⁹So the wine steward said, "In my dream there was a grapevine in front of me ¹⁰with three branches on it. As soon as the leaves came out, the blossoms appeared, and the grapes ripened. ¹¹I was holding the king's cup; so I took the grapes and squeezed them into the cup and gave it to him."

¹²Joseph said, "This is what it means: the three branches are three days. ¹³In three days

---

ᵃPEREZ: *This name in Hebrew means "breaking out."*   ᵇZERAH: *This name sounds like a Hebrew word for the red brightness of dawn.*
39.2 Ac 7.9   **39.21** Ac 7.9

the king will release you, pardon you, and restore you to your position. You will give him his cup as you did before when you were his wine steward. ¹⁴But please remember me when everything is going well for you, and please be kind enough to mention me to the king and help me get out of this prison. ¹⁵After all, I was kidnapped from the land of the Hebrews, and even here in Egypt I didn't do anything to deserve being put in prison."

¹⁶When the chief baker saw that the interpretation of the wine steward's dream was favorable, he said to Joseph, "I had a dream too; I was carrying three breadbaskets on my head. ¹⁷In the top basket there were all kinds of baked goods for the king, and the birds were eating them."

¹⁸Joseph answered, "This is what it means: the three baskets are three days. ¹⁹In three days the king will release you—and have your head cut off! Then he will hang your body on a pole, and the birds will eat your flesh."

²⁰On his birthday three days later the king gave a banquet for all his officials; he released his wine steward and his chief baker and brought them before his officials. ²¹He restored the wine steward to his former position, ²²but he executed the chief baker. It all happened just as Joseph had said. ²³But the wine steward never gave Joseph another thought—he forgot all about him.

Joseph Interprets the King's Dreams

41 After two years had passed, the king of Egypt dreamed that he was standing by the Nile River, ²when seven cows, fat and sleek, came up out of the river and began to feed on the grass. ³Then seven other cows came up; they were thin and bony. They came and stood by the other cows on the riverbank, ⁴and the thin cows ate up the fat cows. Then the king woke up. ⁵He fell asleep again and had another dream. Seven heads of grain, full and ripe, were growing on one stalk. ⁶Then seven other heads of grain sprouted, thin and scorched by the desert wind, ⁷and the thin heads of grain swallowed the full ones. The king woke up and realized that he had been dreaming. ⁸In the morning he was worried, so he sent for all the magicians and wise men of Egypt. He told them his dreams, but no one could explain them to him.

⁹Then the wine steward said to the king, "I must confess today that I have done wrong. ¹⁰You were angry with the chief baker and me, and you put us in prison in the house of the captain of the guard. ¹¹One night each of us had a dream, and the dreams had different meanings. ¹²A young Hebrew was there with us, a slave of the captain of the guard. We told him our dreams, and he interpreted them for us. ¹³Things turned out just as he said: you restored me to my position, but you executed the baker."

¹⁴The king sent for Joseph, and he was immediately brought from the prison. After he had shaved and changed his clothes, he came into the king's presence. ¹⁵The king said to him, "I have had a dream, and no one can explain it. I have been told that you can interpret dreams."

¹⁶Joseph answered, "I cannot, Your Majesty, but God will give a favorable interpretation."

¹⁷The king said, "I dreamed that I was standing on the bank of the Nile, ¹⁸when seven cows, fat and sleek, came up out of the river and began feeding on the grass. ¹⁹Then seven other cows came up which were thin and bony. They were the poorest cows I have ever seen anywhere in Egypt. ²⁰The thin cows ate up the fat ones, ²¹but no one would have known it, because they looked just as bad as before. Then I woke up. ²²I also dreamed that I saw seven heads of grain which were full and ripe, growing on one stalk. ²³Then seven heads of grain sprouted, thin and scorched by the desert wind, ²⁴and the thin heads of grain swallowed the full ones. I told the dreams to the magicians, but none of them could explain them to me."

²⁵Joseph said to the king, "The two dreams mean the same thing; God has told you what he is going to do. ²⁶The seven fat cows are seven years, and the seven full heads of grain are also seven years; they have the same meaning. ²⁷The seven thin cows which came up later and the seven thin heads of grain scorched by the desert wind are seven years of famine. ²⁸It is just as I told you—God has shown you what he is going to do. ²⁹There will be seven

years of great plenty in all the land of Egypt. ³⁰After that, there will be seven years of famine, and all the good years will be forgotten, because the famine will ruin the country. ³¹The time of plenty will be entirely forgotten, because the famine which follows will be so terrible. ³²The repetition of your dream means that the matter is fixed by God and that he will make it happen in the near future.

³³"Now you should choose some man with wisdom and insight and put him in charge of the country. ³⁴You must also appoint other officials and take a fifth of the crops during the seven years of plenty. ³⁵Order them to collect all the food during the good years that are coming, and give them authority to store up grain in the cities and guard it. ³⁶The food will be a reserve supply for the country during the seven years of famine which are going to come on Egypt. In this way the people will not starve."

Joseph Is Made Governor over Egypt

³⁷The king and his officials approved this plan, ³⁸and he said to them, "We will never find a better man than Joseph, a man who has God's spirit in him." ³⁹The king said to Joseph, "God has shown you all this, so it is obvious that you have greater wisdom and insight than anyone else. ⁴⁰I will put you in charge of my country, and all my people will obey your orders. Your authority will be second only to mine. ⁴¹I now appoint you governor over all Egypt." ⁴²The king removed from his finger the ring engraved with the royal seal and put it on Joseph's finger. He put a fine linen robe on him, and placed a gold chain around his neck. ⁴³He gave him the second royal chariot to ride in, and his guard of honor went ahead of him and cried out, "Make way! Make way!" And so Joseph was appointed governor over all Egypt. ⁴⁴The king said to him, "I am the king—and no one in all Egypt shall so much as lift a hand or a foot without your permission." ⁴⁵⁻⁴⁶He gave Joseph the Egyptian name Zaphenath Paneah, and he gave him a wife, Asenath, the daughter of Potiphera, a priest in the city of Heliopolis.

Joseph was thirty years old when he began to serve the king of Egypt. He left the king's court and traveled all over the land. ⁴⁷During the seven years of plenty the land produced abundant crops, ⁴⁸all of which Joseph collected and stored in the cities. In each city he stored the food from the fields around it. ⁴⁹There was so much grain that Joseph stopped measuring it—it was like the sand of the sea.

⁵⁰Before the years of famine came, Joseph had two sons by Asenath. ⁵¹He said, "God has made me forget all my sufferings and all my father's family"; so he named his first son Manasseh.ᵃ ⁵²He also said, "God has given me children in the land of my trouble"; so he named his second son Ephraim.ᵇ

⁵³The seven years of plenty that the land of Egypt had enjoyed came to an end, ⁵⁴and the seven years of famine began, just as Joseph had said. There was famine in every other country, but there was food throughout Egypt. ⁵⁵When the Egyptians began to be hungry, they cried out to the king for food. So he ordered them to go to Joseph and do what he told them. ⁵⁶The famine grew worse and spread over the whole country, so Joseph opened all the storehouses and sold grain to the Egyptians. ⁵⁷People came to Egypt from all over the world to buy grain from Joseph, because the famine was severe everywhere.

Joseph's Brothers Go to Egypt to Buy Grain

42 When Jacob learned that there was grain in Egypt, he said to his sons, "Why don't you do something? ²I hear that there is grain in Egypt; go there and buy some to keep us from starving to death." ³So Joseph's ten half brothers went to buy grain in Egypt, ⁴but Jacob did not send Joseph's full brother Benjamin with them, because he was afraid that something might happen to him.

⁵The sons of Jacob came with others to buy grain, because there was famine in the land of Canaan. ⁶Joseph, as governor of the land of Egypt, was selling grain to people from all over the world. So Joseph's brothers came and bowed down before him with their faces to

---

ᵃMANASSEH: *This name sounds like the Hebrew for "cause to forget."*   ᵇEPHRAIM: *This name sounds like the Hebrew for "give children."*
41.40 Ac 7.10   **41.42** Dn 5.29   **41.54** Ac 7.11   **42.2** Ac 7.12

the ground. [7]When Joseph saw his brothers, he recognized them, but he acted as if he did not know them. He asked them harshly, "Where do you come from?"

"We have come from Canaan to buy food," they answered.

[8]Although Joseph recognized his brothers, they did not recognize him. [9]He remembered the dreams he had dreamed about them and said, "You are spies; you have come to find out where our country is weak."

[10]"No, sir," they answered. "We have come as your slaves, to buy food. [11]We are all brothers. We are not spies, sir, we are honest men."

[12]Joseph said to them, "No! You have come to find out where our country is weak."

[13]They said, "We were twelve brothers in all, sir, sons of the same man in the land of Canaan. One brother is dead, and the youngest is now with our father."

[14]"It is just as I said," Joseph answered. "You are spies. [15]This is how you will be tested: I swear by the name of the king that you will never leave unless your youngest brother comes here. [16]One of you must go and get him. The rest of you will be kept under guard until the truth of what you say can be tested. Otherwise, as sure as the king lives, you are spies." [17]With that, he put them in prison for three days.

[18]On the third day Joseph said to them, "I am a God-fearing man, and I will spare your lives on one condition. [19]To prove that you are honest, one of you will stay in the prison where you have been kept; the rest of you may go and take back to your starving families the grain that you have bought. [20]Then you must bring your youngest brother to me. This will prove that you have been telling the truth, and I will not put you to death."

They agreed to this [21]and said to one another, "Yes, now we are suffering the consequences of what we did to our brother; we saw the great trouble he was in when he begged for help, but we would not listen. That is why we are in this trouble now."

[22]Reuben said, "I told you not to harm the boy, but you wouldn't listen. And now we are being paid back for his death." [23]Joseph understood what they said, but they did not know it, because they had been speaking to him through an interpreter. [24]Joseph left them and began to cry. When he was able to speak again, he came back, picked out Simeon, and had him tied up in front of them.

Joseph's Brothers Return to Canaan

[25]Joseph gave orders to fill his brothers' packs with grain, to put each man's money back in his sack, and to give them food for the trip. This was done. [26]The brothers loaded their donkeys with the grain they had bought, and then they left. [27]At the place where they spent the night, one of them opened his sack to feed his donkey and found his money at the top of the sack. [28]"My money has been returned to me," he called to his brothers. "Here it is in my sack!" Their hearts sank, and in fear they asked one another, "What has God done to us?"

[29]When they came to their father Jacob in Canaan, they told him all that had happened to them: [30]"The governor of Egypt spoke harshly to us and accused us of spying against his country. [31]'We are not spies,' we answered, 'we are honest men. [32]We were twelve brothers in all, sons of the same father. One brother is dead, and the youngest is still in Canaan with our father.' [33]The man answered, 'This is how I will find out if you are honest men: One of you will stay with me; the rest will take grain for your starving families and leave. [34]Bring your youngest brother to me. Then I will know that you are not spies, but honest men; I will give your brother back to you, and you can stay here and trade.' "

[35]Then when they emptied out their sacks, every one of them found his bag of money; and when they saw the money, they and their father Jacob were afraid. [36]Their father said to them, "Do you want to make me lose all my children? Joseph is gone; Simeon is gone; and now you want to take away Benjamin. I am the one who suffers!"

[37]Reuben said to his father, "If I do not bring Benjamin back to you, you can kill my two sons. Put him in my care, and I will bring him back."

[38]But Jacob said, "My son cannot go with you; his brother is dead, and he is the only one left. Something might happen to him on the way. I am an old man, and the sorrow you would cause me would kill me."

42.9 Gn 37.5-10   **42.22** Gn 37.21, 22

Joseph's Brothers Return to Egypt with Benjamin

43 The famine in Canaan got worse, 2and when the family of Jacob had eaten all the grain which had been brought from Egypt, Jacob said to his sons, "Go back and buy a little food for us."

3Judah said to him, "The man sternly warned us that we would not be admitted to his presence unless we had our brother with us. 4If you are willing to send our brother with us, we will go and buy food for you. 5If you are not willing, we will not go, because the man told us we would not be admitted to his presence unless our brother was with us."

6Jacob said, "Why did you cause me so much trouble by telling the man that you had another brother?"

7They answered, "The man kept asking about us and our family, 'Is your father still living? Do you have another brother?' We had to answer his questions. How could we know that he would tell us to bring our brother with us?"

8Judah said to his father, "Send the boy with me, and we will leave at once. Then none of us will starve to death. 9I will pledge my own life, and you can hold me responsible for him. If I do not bring him back to you safe and sound, I will always bear the blame. 10If we had not waited so long, we could have been there and back twice by now."

11Their father said to them, "If that is how it has to be, then take the best products of the land in your packs as a present for the governor: a little resin, a little honey, spices, pistachio nuts, and almonds. 12Take with you also twice as much money, because you must take back the money that was returned in the top of your sacks. Maybe it was a mistake. 13Take your brother and return at once. 14May Almighty God cause the man to have pity on you, so that he will give Benjamin and your other brother back to you. As for me, if I must lose my children, I must lose them."

15So the brothers took the gifts and twice as much money, and set out for Egypt with Benjamin. There they presented themselves to Joseph. 16When Joseph saw Benjamin with them, he said to the servant in charge of his house, "Take these men to my house. They are going to eat with me at noon, so kill an animal and prepare it." 17The servant did as he was commanded and took the brothers to Joseph's house.

18As they were being brought to Joseph's house, they were afraid and thought, "We are being brought here because of the money that was returned in our sacks the first time. They will suddenly attack us, take our donkeys, and make us his slaves." 19So at the door of the house, they said to the servant in charge, 20"If you please, sir, we came here once before to buy food. 21When we set up camp on the way home, we opened our sacks, and each man found his money in the top of his sack—every bit of it. We have brought it back to you. 22We have also brought some more money with us to buy more food. We do not know who put our money back in our sacks."

23The servant said, "Don't worry. Don't be afraid. Your God, the God of your father, must have put the money in your sacks for you. I received your payment." Then he brought Simeon to them.

24The servant took the brothers into the house. He gave them water so that they could wash their feet, and he fed their donkeys. 25They got their gifts ready to present to Joseph when he arrived at noon, because they had been told that they were to eat with him. 26When Joseph got home, they took the gifts into the house to him and bowed down to the ground before him. 27He asked about their health and then said, "You told me about your old father—how is he? Is he still alive and well?"

28They answered, "Your humble servant, our father, is still alive and well." And they knelt and bowed down before him.

29When Joseph saw his brother Benjamin, he said, "So this is your youngest brother, the one you told me about. God bless you, my son." 30Then Joseph left suddenly, because his heart was full of tender feelings for his brother. He was about to break down, so he went to his room and cried. 31After he had washed his face, he came out, and controlling himself, he ordered the meal to be served. 32Joseph was served at one table and his brothers at another. The Egyptians who were eating there were served separately, because they considered it beneath their dignity to eat with Hebrews. 33The brothers had been seated at the table, facing Joseph, in the order of their age from the oldest to the youngest. When they saw how they had been seated, they looked at one another in amazement. ³⁴Food was served to them from Joseph's table, and Benjamin was served five times as much as the rest of them. So they ate and drank with Joseph until they were drunk.

The Missing Cup

44 Joseph commanded the servant in charge of his house, "Fill the men's sacks with as much food as they can carry, and put each man's money in the top of his sack. ²Put my silver cup in the top of the youngest brother's sack, together with the money for his grain." He did as he was told. ³Early in the morning the brothers were sent on their way with their donkeys. ⁴When they had gone only a short distance from the city, Joseph said to the servant in charge of his house, "Hurry after those men. When you catch up with them, ask them, 'Why have you paid back evil for good? ⁵Why did you steal my master's silver cup?ᵃ It is the one he drinks from, the one he uses for divination. You have committed a serious crime!' "

⁶When the servant caught up with them, he repeated these words. ⁷They answered him, "What do you mean, sir, by talking like this? We swear that we have done no such thing. ⁸You know that we brought back to you from the land of Canaan the money we found in the top of our sacks. Why then should we steal silver or gold from your master's house? ⁹Sir, if any one of us is found to have it, he will be put to death, and the rest of us will become your slaves."

¹⁰He said, "I agree; but only the one who has taken the cup will become my slave, and the rest of you can go free." ¹¹So they quickly lowered their sacks to the ground, and each man opened his sack. ¹²Joseph's servant searched carefully, beginning with the oldest and ending with the youngest, and the cup was found in Benjamin's sack. ¹³The brothers tore their clothes in sorrow, loaded their donkeys, and returned to the city.

¹⁴When Judah and his brothers came to Joseph's house, he was still there. They bowed down before him, ¹⁵and Joseph said, "What have you done? Didn't you know that a man in my position could find you out by practicing divination?"

¹⁶"What can we say to you, sir?" Judah answered. "How can we argue? How can we clear ourselves? God has uncovered our guilt. All of us are now your slaves and not just the one with whom the cup was found."

¹⁷Joseph said, "Oh, no! I would never do that! Only the one who had the cup will be my slave. The rest of you may go back safe and sound to your father."

Judah Pleads for Benjamin

¹⁸Judah went up to Joseph and said, "Please, sir, allow me to speak with you freely. Don't be angry with me; you are like the king himself. ¹⁹Sir, you asked us, 'Do you have a father or another brother?' ²⁰We answered, 'We have a father who is old and a younger brother, born to him in his old age. The boy's brother is dead, and he is the only one of his mother's children still alive; his father loves him very much.' ²¹Sir, you told us to bring him here, so that you could see him, ²²and we answered that the boy could not leave his father; if he did, his father would die. ²³Then you said, 'You will not be admitted to my presence again unless your youngest brother comes with you.'

²⁴"When we went back to our father, we told him what you had said. ²⁵Then he told us to return and buy a little food. ²⁶We answered, 'We cannot go; we will not be admitted to the man's presence unless our youngest brother is with us. We can go only if our youngest brother goes also.' ²⁷Our father said to us, 'You know that my wife Rachel bore me only two sons. ²⁸One of them has already left me. He must have been torn to pieces by wild animals, because I have not seen him since he left. ²⁹If you take this one from me now and something happens to him, the sorrow you would cause me would kill me, as old as I am.'

³⁰⁻³¹"And now, sir," Judah continued, "if I go back to my father without the boy, as soon as he sees that the boy is not with me, he will die. His life is wrapped up with the life of the boy, and he is so old that the sorrow we would cause him would kill him. ³²What is more, I pledged my life to my father for the boy. I told him that if I did not bring the boy back to him, I would bear the blame all my life. ³³And now, sir, I will stay here as your slave in place of the boy; let him go back with his brothers. ³⁴How can I go back to my father if the boy is not with me? I cannot bear to see this disaster come upon my father."

ᵃOne ancient translation Why did you steal my master's silver cup?; Hebrew does not have these words.

Joseph Tells His Brothers Who He Is

45 Joseph was no longer able to control his feelings in front of his servants, so he ordered them all to leave the room. No one else was with him when Joseph told his brothers who he was. [2]He cried with such loud sobs that the Egyptians heard it, and the news was taken to the king's palace. [3]Joseph said to his brothers, "I am Joseph. Is my father still alive?" But when his brothers heard this, they were so terrified that they could not answer. [4]Then Joseph said to them, "Please come closer." They did, and he said, "I am your brother Joseph, whom you sold into Egypt. [5]Now do not be upset or blame yourselves because you sold me here. It was really God who sent me ahead of you to save people's lives. [6]This is only the second year of famine in the land; there will be five more years in which there will be neither plowing nor reaping. [7]God sent me ahead of you to rescue you in this amazing way and to make sure that you and your descendants survive. [8]So it was not really you who sent me here, but God. He has made me the king's highest official. I am in charge of his whole country; I am the ruler of all Egypt.

[9]"Now hurry back to my father and tell him that this is what his son Joseph says: 'God has made me ruler of all Egypt; come to me without delay. [10]You can live in the region of Goshen, where you can be near me—you, your children, your grandchildren, your sheep, your goats, your cattle, and everything else that you have. [11]If you are in Goshen, I can take care of you. There will still be five years of famine; and I do not want you, your family, and your livestock to starve.' "

[12]Joseph continued, "Now all of you, and you too, Benjamin, can see that I am really Joseph. [13]Tell my father how powerful I am here in Egypt and tell him about everything that you have seen. Then hurry and bring him here."

[14]He threw his arms around his brother Benjamin and began to cry; Benjamin also cried as he hugged him. [15]Then, still weeping, he embraced each of his brothers and kissed them. After that, his brothers began to talk with him.

[16]When the news reached the palace that Joseph's brothers had come, the king and his officials were pleased. [17]He said to Joseph, "Tell your brothers to load their animals and to return to the land of Canaan. [18]Let them get their father and their families and come back here. I will give them the best land in Egypt, and they will have more than enough to live on. [19]Tell them also to take wagons with them from Egypt for their wives and small children and to bring their father with them. [20]They are not to worry about leaving their possessions behind; the best in the whole land of Egypt will be theirs."

[21]Jacob's sons did as they were told. Joseph gave them wagons, as the king had ordered, and food for the trip. [22]He also gave each of them a change of clothes, but he gave Benjamin three hundred pieces of silver and five changes of clothes. [23]He sent his father ten donkeys loaded with the best Egyptian goods and ten donkeys loaded with grain, bread, and other food for the trip. [24]He sent his brothers off and as they left, he said to them, "Don't quarrel on the way."

[25]They left Egypt and went back home to their father Jacob in Canaan. [26]"Joseph is still alive!" they told him. "He is the ruler of all Egypt!" Jacob was stunned and could not believe them.

[27]But when they told him all that Joseph had said to them, and when he saw the wagons which Joseph had sent to take him to Egypt, he recovered from the shock. [28]"My son Joseph is still alive!" he said. "This is all I could ask for! I must go and see him before I die."

Jacob and His Family Go to Egypt

46 Jacob packed up all he had and went to Beersheba, where he offered sacrifices to the God of his father Isaac. [2]God spoke to him in a vision at night and called, "Jacob, Jacob!"

"Yes, here I am," he answered.

[3]"I am God, the God of your father," he said. "Do not be afraid to go to Egypt; I will make your descendants a great nation there. [4]I will go with you to Egypt, and I will bring your descendants back to this land. Joseph will be with you when you die."

45.1 Ac 7.13   **45.9-11** Ac 7.14

⁵Jacob set out from Beersheba. His sons put him, their small children, and their wives in the wagons which the king of Egypt had sent. ⁶They took their livestock and the possessions they had acquired in Canaan and went to Egypt. Jacob took all his descendants with him: ⁷his sons, his grandsons, his daughters, and his granddaughters.

⁸The members of Jacob's family who went to Egypt with him were his oldest son Reuben ⁹and Reuben's sons: Hanoch, Pallu, Hezron, and Carmi. ¹⁰Simeon and his sons: Jemuel, Jamin, Ohad, Jachin, Zohar, and Shaul, the son of a Canaanite woman. ¹¹Levi and his sons: Gershon, Kohath, and Merari. ¹²Judah and his sons: Shelah, Perez, and Zerah. (Judah's other sons, Er and Onan, had died in Canaan.) Perez' sons were Hezron and Hamul. ¹³Issachar and his sons: Tola, Puah, Jashub, and Shimron. ¹⁴Zebulun and his sons: Sered, Elon, and Jahleel. ¹⁵These are the sons that Leah had borne to Jacob in Mesopotamia, besides his daughter Dinah. In all, his descendants by Leah numbered thirty-three.

¹⁶Gad and his sons: Zephon, Haggi, Shuni, Ezbon, Eri, Arod, and Areli. ¹⁷Asher and his sons: Imnah, Ishvah, Ishvi, Beriah, and their sister Serah. Beriah's sons were Heber and Malchiel. ¹⁸These sixteen are the descendants of Jacob by Zilpah, the slave woman whom Laban gave to his daughter Leah.

¹⁹Jacob's wife Rachel bore him two sons: Joseph and Benjamin. ²⁰In Egypt Joseph had two sons, Manasseh and Ephraim, by Asenath, the daughter of Potiphera, a priest in Heliopolis. ²¹Benjamin's sons were Bela, Becher, Ashbel, Gera, Naaman, Ehi, Rosh, Muppim, Huppim, and Ard. ²²These fourteen are the descendants of Jacob by Rachel.

²³Dan and his son Hushim. ²⁴Naphtali and his sons: Jahzeel, Guni, Jezer, and Shillem. ²⁵These seven are the descendants of Jacob by Bilhah, the slave woman whom Laban gave to his daughter Rachel.

²⁶The total number of the direct descendants of Jacob who went to Egypt was sixty-six, not including his sons' wives. ²⁷Two sons were born to Joseph in Egypt, bringing to seventy the total number of Jacob's family who went there.

Jacob and His Family in Egypt

²⁸Jacob sent Judah ahead to ask Joseph to meet them in Goshen. When they arrived, ²⁹Joseph got in his chariot and went to Goshen to meet his father. When they met, Joseph threw his arms around his father's neck and cried for a long time. ³⁰Jacob said to Joseph, "I am ready to die, now that I have seen you and know that you are still alive."

³¹Then Joseph said to his brothers and the rest of his father's family, "I must go and tell the king that my brothers and all my father's family, who were living in Canaan, have come to me. ³²I will tell him that you are shepherds and take care of livestock and that you have brought your flocks and herds and everything else that belongs to you. ³³When the king calls for you and asks what your occupation is, ³⁴be sure to tell him that you have taken care of livestock all your lives, just as your ancestors did. In this way he will let you live in the region of Goshen." Joseph said this because Egyptians will have nothing to do with shepherds.

47 So Joseph took five of his brothers and went to the king. He told him, "My father and my brothers have come from Canaan with their flocks, their herds, and all that they own. They are now in the region of Goshen." ²He then presented his brothers to the king. ³The king asked them, "What is your occupation?"

"We are shepherds, sir, just as our ancestors were," they answered. ⁴"We have come to live in this country, because in the land of Canaan the famine is so severe that there is no pasture for our flocks. Please give us permission to live in the region of Goshen." ⁵The king said to Joseph, "Now that your father and your brothers have arrived, ⁶the land of Egypt is theirs. Let them settle in the region of Goshen, the best part of the land. And if there are any capable men among them, put them in charge of my own livestock."

⁷Then Joseph brought his father Jacob and presented him to the king. Jacob gave the king his blessing, ⁸and the king asked him, "How old are you?"

⁹Jacob answered, "My life of wandering has lasted a hundred and thirty years. Those years have been few and difficult, unlike the long years of my ancestors in their wanderings." ¹⁰Jacob gave the king a farewell blessing and left. ¹¹Then Joseph settled his father and his broth-

46.6 Ac 7.15   **46.20** Gn 41.50-52   **46.27** Ac 7.14

ers in Egypt, giving them property in the best of the land near the city of Rameses, as the king had commanded. 12Joseph provided food for his father, his brothers, and all the rest of his father's family, including the very youngest.

The Famine

13The famine was so severe that there was no food anywhere, and the people of Egypt and Canaan became weak with hunger. 14As they bought grain, Joseph collected all the money and took it to the palace. 15When all the money in Egypt and Canaan was spent, the Egyptians came to Joseph and said, "Give us food! Don't let us die. Do something! Our money is all gone."

16Joseph answered, "Bring your livestock; I will give you food in exchange for it if your money is all gone." 17So they brought their livestock to Joseph, and he gave them food in exchange for their horses, sheep, goats, cattle, and donkeys. That year he supplied them with food in exchange for all their livestock.

18The following year they came to him and said, "We will not hide the fact from you, sir, that our money is all gone and our livestock belongs to you. There is nothing left to give you except our bodies and our lands. 19Don't let us die. Do something! Don't let our fields be deserted. Buy us and our land in exchange for food. We will be the king's slaves, and he will own our land. Give us grain to keep us alive and seed so that we can plant our fields."

20Joseph bought all the land in Egypt for the king. Every Egyptian was forced to sell his land, because the famine was so severe; and all the land became the king's property. 21Joseph made slaves of the people from one end of Egypt to the other. 22The only land he did not buy was the land that belonged to the priests. They did not have to sell their lands, because the king gave them an allowance to live on. 23Joseph said to the people, "You see, I have now bought you and your lands for the king. Here is seed for you to sow in your fields. 24At the time of harvest you must give one-fifth to the king. You can use the rest for seed and for food for yourselves and your families."

25They answered, "You have saved our lives; you have been good to us, sir, and we will be the king's slaves." 26So Joseph made it a law for the land of Egypt that one-fifth of the harvest should belong to the king. This law still remains in force today. Only the lands of the priests did not become the king's property.

Jacob's Last Request

27The Israelites lived in Egypt in the region of Goshen, where they became rich and had many children. 28Jacob lived in Egypt seventeen years, until he was a hundred and forty-seven years old. 29When the time drew near for him to die, he called for his son Joseph and said to him, "Place your hand between my thighsa and make a solemn vow that you will not bury me in Egypt. 30I want to be buried where my fathers are; carry me out of Egypt and bury me where they are buried."

Joseph answered, "I will do as you say."

31Jacob said, "Make a vow that you will." Joseph made the vow, and Jacob gave thanks there on his bed.

Jacob Blesses Ephraim and Manasseh

48 Some time later Joseph was told that his father was ill. So he took his two sons, Manasseh and Ephraim, and went to see Jacob. 2When Jacob was told that his son Joseph had come to see him, he gathered his strength and sat up in bed. 3Jacob said to Joseph, "Almighty God appeared to me at Luz in the land of Canaan and blessed me. 4He said to me, 'I will give you many children, so that your descendants will become many nations; I will give this land to your descendants as their possession forever.' "

5Jacob continued, "Joseph, your two sons, who were born to you in Egypt before I came here, belong to me; Ephraim and Manasseh are just as much my sons as Reuben and Simeon. 6If you have any more sons, they will not be considered mine; the inheritance they get will come through Ephraim and Manasseh. 7I am doing this because of your mother Rachel. To my great sorrow she died in the land of Canaan, not far from Ephrath, as I was returning

aPLACE . . . THIGHS: See 24.2.
47.29, 30 Gn 49.29-32; 50.6   **48.3, 4** Gn 28.13, 14   **48.7** Gn 35.16-19

from Mesopotamia. I buried her there beside the road to Ephrath." (Ephrath is now known as Bethlehem.)

8When Jacob saw Joseph's sons, he asked, "Who are these boys?"

9Joseph answered, "These are my sons, whom God has given me here in Egypt."

Jacob said, "Bring them to me so that I may bless them." 10Jacob's eyesight was failing because of his age, and he could not see very well. Joseph brought the boys to him, and he hugged them and kissed them. 11Jacob said to Joseph, "I never expected to see you again, and now God has even let me see your children." 12Then Joseph took them from Jacob's lap and bowed down before him with his face to the ground.

13Joseph put Ephraim at Jacob's left and Manasseh at his right. 14But Jacob crossed his hands, and put his right hand on the head of Ephraim, even though he was the younger, and his left hand on the head of Manasseh, who was the older. 15Then he blessed Joseph:[a]

> "May God, whom my fathers Abraham
>   and Isaac served, bless these
>   boys!
> May God, who has led me to this very
>   day, bless them!
> 16May the angel, who has rescued me
>   from all harm, bless them!
> May my name and the name of my
>   fathers Abraham and Isaac live on
>   through these boys!
> May they have many children, many
>   descendants!"

"May God . . . bless these boys!" (48.15)

17Joseph was upset when he saw that his father had put his right hand on Ephraim's head; so he took his father's hand to move it from Ephraim's head to the head of Manasseh. 18He said to his father, "Not that way, father. This is the older boy; put your right hand on his head."

19His father refused, saying, "I know, son, I know. Manasseh's descendants will also become a great people. But his younger brother will be greater than he, and his descendants will become great nations."

20So he blessed them that day, saying, "The Israelites will use your names when they pronounce blessings. They will say, 'May God make you like Ephraim and Manasseh.' " In this way Jacob put Ephraim before Manasseh.

21Then Jacob said to Joseph, "As you see, I am about to die, but God will be with you and will take you back to the land of your ancestors. 22It is to you and not to your brothers that I am giving Shechem, that fertile region which I took from the Amorites with my sword and my bow."

The Last Words of Jacob

49 Jacob called for his sons and said, "Gather around, and I will tell you what will happen to you in the future:

> 2"Come together and listen, sons of Jacob.
>   Listen to your father Israel.

> 3"Reuben, my first-born, you are my strength
>   And the first child of my manhood,
>   The proudest and strongest of all my sons.
> 4You are like a raging flood,
>   But you will not be the most important,

[a]JOSEPH: *In blessing Ephraim and Manasseh, Jacob was in fact blessing Joseph.*
48.20 He 11.21

For you slept with my concubine
And dishonored your father's bed.

5"Simeon and Levi are brothers.
They use their weapons to commit violence.
6I will not join in their secret talks,
Nor will I take part in their meetings,
For they killed people in anger
And they crippled bulls for sport.
7A curse be on their anger, because it is so fierce,
And on their fury, because it is so cruel.
I will scatter them throughout the land of Israel.
I will disperse them among its people.

8"Judah, your brothers will praise you.
You hold your enemies by the neck.
Your brothers will bow down before you.
9Judah is like a lion,
Killing his victim and returning to his den,
Stretching out and lying down.
No one dares disturb him.
10Judah will hold the royal scepter,
And his descendants will always rule.
Nations will bring him tribute*a*
And bow in obedience before him.
11He ties his young donkey to a grapevine,
To the very best of the vines.
He washes his clothes in blood-red wine.
12His eyes are bloodshot from drinking wine,
His teeth white from drinking milk.*b*

13"Zebulun will live beside the sea.
His shore will be a haven for ships.
His territory will reach as far as Sidon.

14"Issachar is no better than a donkey
That lies stretched out between its saddlebags.
15But he sees that the resting place is good
And that the land is delightful.
So he bends his back to carry the load
And is forced to work as a slave.

16"Dan will be a ruler for his people.
They will be like the other tribes of Israel.
17Dan will be a snake at the side of the road,
A poisonous snake beside the path,
That strikes at the horse's heel,
So that the rider is thrown off backward.

18"I wait for your deliverance, LORD.

19"Gad will be attacked by a band of robbers,
But he will turn and pursue them.

*a*Probable text Nations . . . tribute; Hebrew unclear.   *b*His eyes . . . milk; or His eyes are darker than wine,
his teeth are whiter than milk.
49.9 Nu 24.9; Rev 5.5

20"Asher's land will produce rich food.
He will provide food fit for a king.

21"Naphtali is a deer that runs free,
Who bears lovely fawns.ª

22"Joseph is like a wild donkey by a spring,
A wild colt on a hillside.ᵇ
23His enemies attack him fiercely
And pursue him with their bows and arrows.
24But his bow remains steady,
And his arms are made strongᶜ
By the power of the Mighty God of Jacob,
By the Shepherd, the Protector of Israel.
25It is your father's God who helps you,
The Almighty God who blesses you
With blessings of rain from above
And of deep waters from beneath the ground,
Blessings of many cattle and children,
26Blessings of grain and flowers,ᵈ
Blessings of ancient mountains,ᵉ
Delightful things from everlasting hills.
May these blessings rest on the head of Joseph,
On the brow of the one set apart from his brothers.

27"Benjamin is like a vicious wolf.
Morning and evening he kills and devours."

28These are the twelve tribes of Israel, and this is what their father said as he spoke a suitable word of farewell to each son.

The Death and Burial of Jacob

29Then Jacob commanded his sons, "Now that I am going to join my people in death, bury me with my fathers in the cave that is in the field of Ephron the Hittite, 30at Machpelah east of Mamre in the land of Canaan. Abraham bought this cave and field from Ephron for a burial ground. 31That is where they buried Abraham and his wife Sarah; that is where they buried Isaac and his wife Rebecca; and that is where I buried Leah. 32The field and the cave in it were bought from the Hittites. Bury me there." 33When Jacob had finished giving instructions to his sons, he lay back down and died.

50 Joseph threw himself on his father, crying and kissing his face. 2Then Joseph gave orders to embalm his father's body. 3It took forty days, the normal time for embalming. The Egyptians mourned for him seventy days.

4When the time of mourning was over, Joseph said to the king's officials, "Please take this message to the king: 5'When my father was about to die, he made me promise him that I would bury him in the tomb which he had prepared in the land of Canaan. So please let me go and bury my father, and then I will come back.' "

6The king answered, "Go and bury your father, as you promised you would."

7So Joseph went to bury his father. All the king's officials, the senior men of his court, and all the leading men of Egypt went with Joseph. 8His family, his brothers, and the rest of his father's family all went with him. Only their small children and their sheep, goats, and cattle stayed in the region of Goshen. 9Men in chariots and men on horseback also went with him; it was a huge group.

ªNaphtali . . . fawns; or Naphtali is a spreading tree that puts out lovely branches.   ᵇJoseph . . . hillside; or Joseph is like a tree by a spring, a fruitful tree that spreads over a wall.   ᶜBut . . . strong; or But their bows were broken and splintered, the muscles of their arms torn apart.   ᵈProbable text grain and flowers; Hebrew your fathers are mightier than.   ᵉOne ancient translation ancient mountains; Hebrew my ancestors to.
49.30 Gn 23.3-20   **49.31** a Gn 25.9, 10; b Gn 35.29   **49.33** Ac 7.15   **50.5** Gn 47.29-31

54 GENESIS 50

10When they came to the threshing place at Atad east of the Jordan, they mourned loudly for a long time, and Joseph performed mourning ceremonies for seven days. **11**When the citizens of Canaan saw those people mourning at Atad, they said, "What a solemn ceremony of mourning the Egyptians are holding!" That is why the place was named Abel Mizraim.[a]

12So Jacob's sons did as he had commanded them; **13**they carried his body to Canaan and buried it in the cave at Machpelah east of Mamre in the field which Abraham had bought from Ephron the Hittite for a burial ground. **14**After Joseph had buried his father, he returned to Egypt with his brothers and all who had gone with him for the funeral.

Joseph Reassures His Brothers

15After the death of their father, Joseph's brothers said, "What if Joseph still hates us and plans to pay us back for all the harm we did to him?" **16**So they sent a message to Joseph: "Before our father died, **17**he told us to ask you, 'Please forgive the crime your brothers committed when they wronged you.' Now please forgive us the wrong that we, the servants of your father's God, have done." Joseph cried when he received this message.

18Then his brothers themselves came and bowed down before him. "Here we are before you as your slaves," they said.

19But Joseph said to them, "Don't be afraid; I can't put myself in the place of God. **20**You plotted evil against me, but God turned it into good, in order to preserve the lives of many people who are alive today because of what happened. **21**You have nothing to fear. I will take care of you and your children." So he reassured them with kind words that touched their hearts.

The Death of Joseph

22Joseph continued to live in Egypt with his father's family; he was a hundred and ten years old when he died. **23**He lived to see Ephraim's children and grandchildren. He also lived to receive the children of Machir son of Manasseh into the family. **24**He said to his brothers, "I am about to die, but God will certainly take care of you and lead you out of this land to the land he solemnly promised to Abraham, Isaac, and Jacob." **25**Then Joseph asked his people to make a vow. "Promise me," he said, "that when God leads you to that land, you will take my body with you." **26**So Joseph died in Egypt at the age of a hundred and ten. They embalmed his body and put it in a coffin.

[a]ABEL MIZRAIM: *This name sounds like the Hebrew for "mourning of the Egyptians."*
50.13 Ac 7.16 **50.25** Ex 13.19; Js 24.32; He 11.22

Exodus

Introduction

The name Exodus means "departure" and refers to the most important event in Israel's history, which is described in this book—the departure of the people of Israel from Egypt, where they had been slaves. The book has four main parts: 1) the freeing of the Hebrews from slavery; 2) their journey to Mount Sinai; 3) God's covenant with his people at Sinai, which gave them moral, civil, and religious laws to live by; and 4) the building and furnishing of a place of worship for Israel, and laws regarding the priests and the worship of God.

Above all, this book describes what God did, as he liberated his enslaved people and formed them into a nation with hope for the future.

The central human figure in the book is Moses, the man whom God chose to lead his people from Egypt. The most widely known part of the book is the list of the Ten Commandments in chapter 20.

Outline of Contents

The Israelites Are Treated Cruelly in Egypt

1 The sons of Jacob who went to Egypt with him, each with his family, were [2]Reuben, Simeon, Levi, Judah, [3]Issachar, Zebulun, Benjamin, [4]Dan, Naphtali, Gad, and Asher. [5]The total number of these people directly descended from Jacob was seventy.[a] His son Joseph was already in Egypt. [6]In the course of time Joseph, his brothers, and all the rest of that generation died, [7]but their descendants, the Israelites, had many children and became so numerous and strong that Egypt was filled with them.

[8]Then, a new king, who knew nothing about Joseph, came to power in Egypt. [9]He said to his people, "These Israelites are so numerous and strong that they are a threat to us. [10]In case of war they might join our enemies in order to fight against us, and might escape from[b] the country. We must find some way to keep them from becoming even more numerous." [11]So the Egyptians put slave drivers over them to crush their spirits with hard labor. The Israelites built the cities of Pithom and Rameses to serve as supply centers for the king. [12]But the more the Egyptians oppressed the Israelites, the more they increased in number and the farther they spread through the land. The Egyptians came to fear the Israelites [13-14]and made their lives miserable by forcing them into cruel slavery. They made them work on their building projects and in their fields, and they had no pity on them.

[15]Then the king of Egypt spoke to Shiphrah and Puah, the two midwives who helped the Hebrew women. [16]"When you help the Hebrew women give birth," he said to them, "kill the baby if it is a boy; but if it is a girl, let it live." [17]But the midwives were God-fearing and so

---

[a]One ancient translation seventy-five (see Ac 7.14).   [b]escape from; or take control of.
1.1-4 Gn 46.8-27   **1.7** Ac 7.17   **1.8** Ac 7.18   **1.10** Ac 7.19

did not obey the king; instead, they let the boys live. [18]So the king sent for the midwives and asked them, "Why are you doing this? Why are you letting the boys live?"

[19]They answered, "The Hebrew women are not like Egyptian women; they give birth easily, and their babies are born before either of us gets there." [20-21]Because the midwives were God-fearing, God was good to them and gave them families of their own. And the Israelites continued to increase and become strong. [22]Finally the king issued a command to all his people: "Take every newborn Hebrew boy and throw him into the Nile, but let all the girls live."

The Birth of Moses

2 During this time a man from the tribe of Levi married a woman of his own tribe, [2]and she bore him a son. When she saw what a fine baby he was, she hid him for three months. [3]But when she could not hide him any longer, she took a basket made of reeds and covered it with tar to make it watertight. She put the baby in it and then placed it in the tall grass at the edge of the river. [4]The baby's sister stood some distance away to see what would happen to him.

[5]The king's daughter came down to the river to bathe, while her servants walked along the bank. Suddenly she noticed the basket in the tall grass and sent a slave woman to get it. [6]The princess opened it and saw a baby boy. He was crying, and she felt sorry for him. "This is one of the Hebrew babies," she said.

[7]Then his sister asked her, "Shall I go and call a Hebrew woman to nurse the baby for you?"

[8]"Please do," she answered. So the girl went and brought the baby's own mother.

The king's daughter . . . noticed the basket. (2.5)

[9]The princess told the woman, "Take this baby and nurse him for me, and I will pay you." So she took the baby and nursed him. [10]Later, when the child was old enough, she took him to the king's daughter, who adopted him as her own son. She said to herself, "I pulled him out of the water, and so I name him Moses."[a]

Moses Escapes to Midian

[11]When Moses had grown up, he went out to visit his people, the Hebrews, and he saw how they were forced to do hard labor. He even saw an Egyptian kill a Hebrew, one of Moses' own people. [12]Moses looked all around, and when he saw that no one was watching, he killed the Egyptian and hid his body in the sand. [13]The next day he went back and saw two Hebrew men fighting. He said to the one who was in the wrong, "Why are you beating up a fellow Hebrew?"

[14]The man answered, "Who made you our ruler and judge? Are you going to kill me just as you killed that Egyptian?" Then Moses was afraid and said to himself, "People have found out what I have done." [15-16]When the king heard about what had happened, he tried to have Moses killed, but Moses fled and went to live in the land of Midian.

One day, when Moses was sitting by a well, seven daughters of Jethro, the priest of Midian, came to draw water and fill the troughs for their father's sheep and goats. [17]But some shepherds drove Jethro's daughters away. Then Moses went to their rescue and watered their animals for them. [18]When they returned to their father, he asked, "Why have you come back so early today?"

[19]"An Egyptian rescued us from the shepherds," they answered, "and he even drew water for us and watered our animals."

[20]"Where is he?" he asked his daughters. "Why did you leave the man out there? Go and invite him to eat with us."

[a]MOSES: *This name sounds like the Hebrew for "pull out."*
1.22 Ac 7.19   **2.2** Ac 7.20; He 11.23   **2.10** Ac 7.21   **2.11-14** Ac 7.23-28   **2.11** He 11.24   **2.15** Ac 7.29; He 11.27